THE
CITY

THE CITY

STORIES

J. W. Du Four

Published 2025
by J. W. Du Four

ISBN 978-0-473-76128-8 (International Edition)

COPYPRESS

Designed and distributed in New Zealand by CopyPress, Nelson, New Zealand.

www.copypress.co.nz

For Sue

'The streets of London have their map, but our passions are uncharted. What are you going to meet if you turn this corner?' – Virginia Woolf

CONTENTS

THE MARKET. 1

THE PARK 19

THE UNDERGROUND. . . . 29

THE HEATH 41

THE GARDEN 53

THE MUSEUM 63

THE PUB 75

THE CATHEDRAL 91

THE ESTATE 105

THE HOLIDAY 121

THE WHARF 137

THE MARKET

FAEY EMERGES FROM the underground and is immediately picked up and swept northwards towards the locks by the sea of bodies surging along the rise of Camden High Street. Her bobbing head stands out from the crowd, even here, where all types rub shoulders and nothing is too strange.

It's her black hair. Not just any black, but a shimmering jet-black-blacker-than-black-so-black-it-borders-on-blue-black. The severe fringe dissects her forehead in a picture-perfect slash, a horizontal lobotomy, while midnight sheen tumbles away to either side in a ruler-straight coal-fall sheered off just above the base of her slender neck.

In vivid contrast to the hair is her white-powdered face, a startling death mask that is somehow intensely alive. It is lifted from the grave by soft, smoky-green eyes, the colour of water-worn pounamu, sacred jade-stone of the indigenous Maori in her far-off New Zealand homeland.

Her wide-set eyes lend her gaze a beguiling innocence, contrasting with the trio of titanium circlets burrowing and overlapping their way along the outer halves of each thin eyebrow. Her mouth is small and sweet, but her lips are painted a startling vampish red, locked in by a thin rim of black.

What grabs the attention next is her clothing. She is swathed in black layers of it, hiding into itself, spilling from pallid neck down boyish front and slender hips: shawl over shirt, over mid-length dress, over skin-tight denims, arms bound tight and narrow with ribbon, finishing in lace across the back of pale hands. She marches to the scuffling beat of her Doc Martins and the rhythmic swing of various black-beaded necklaces. A gothic harmony; a union of Victoriana, hippy, bovver boy and funeral director.

Faey works in the market, Canal Market to be precise: the smallest of the myriad markets scattering the length and breadth of Camden Town. Her tiny stall sits at the end of a single long passageway containing a rag-tag collection of a hundred-and-fifty shops and stalls, selling everything from fashion accessories to recorded music, computer games to clothing, jewellery to gifts and collectables.

And predictions. For Faey is a psychic. A medium. A seer. She scries soul paths and prophesies life's probabilities for those who pay their twenty-five pounds to sit at her table and open themselves to possibility. Behind beaded curtains, beneath posters and wall hangings that depict wolves howling at the moon, white unicorns in dark forests, and dragons flying far above ancient stone circles, the punters sit: surrounded by the dancing glow of candles, crystal geodes, small carved goddesses, and wafting sticks of fragrant amber and cedarwood.

Faey is a Sun Scorpio, Aquarius Ascendant. Faey is a vegan. Faey strikes singing bowls and tingsha bells. Faey understands that according to the Wisdom Elders of the Andes these are the days of Pachacuti – a time of transformation, when the Earth and the cosmos are turned upside down.

And one other thing: Faey is a fake.

She makes her way past Inverness Street and Jamestown Road, up over Regents Canal and down to the right, where she enters a covered tunnel and is immediately enveloped by the smells of an array of international street-food stalls: sharp, cloying, pungent, savoury – an olfactory blur that confuses and entices in equal measure.

'Hello, Faey!' comes a shout from behind an enormous steaming wok.

Faey walks over and smiles. 'Gidday, Lucy.'

With strong, short arms and wielding a metal scoop, Lucy Wong is digging in and flipping a tangled nest of noodles, flecked with yellow egg, green peas, orange carrot and pink shrimp.

'You starting late today! Sleep in, you lazy-head?'

'No,' says Faey. 'I had to go to the post office to send a pressie home for my nephew.' She looks around. 'Think it'll be a busy day?'

'You tell me – you the fortune teller,' says Lucy.

Faey laughs. 'I see lots of chow mein in your future.'

'Gee, you good!' says Lucy. 'I bring you pork bun later, maybe siu mai, too, eh?'

'That'd be great!' says Faey, waving as she heads off down the long sloping passage towards her stall. Reggae music crashes out to her right, clashing and combining with a crooning Tony Bennett from the shop opposite in a duet that somehow seems to work. Faey pokes her head in DaRastaShack and shouts, 'Hi ya, Bennie!' From below the counter a booming black voice burrows its way up from under the sunny Jamaican soundscape: 'Morning to you, Faey-child. Or should I say "afternoon"?' Faey rolls her eyes and continues on her way.

Reaching the end of the walkway, she comes to her makeshift doorway of long elder branches. They are lashed together with a weaving twist of her homeland's farming fix-all, Number 8 fence wire, a touch of Kiwiana that never fails to bring a smile to her lips. She unfastens the small padlock and enters.

Rubbing her hands against the chill, Faey first turns on a small fan-heater sitting beneath the round table covered with heavy black velvet – having your punters shivering is never good for business. She plugs in the electric kettle, and then sets about lighting the many tea-lights and other candles positioned around the small space, finishing with the large red one in the very centre of the table. Next, she lights her incense.

Water boiled, she makes herself a cup of chamomile tea, wrapping her cold fingers around the heat of the chipped mug. She bends down and pushes play on the bashed old cassette player stowed behind her chair. Ambient new age music washes around her: swirly, swishy synth-sounds that help to create atmosphere and block out the market din beyond her gate.

Faey hears a musical ping from inside her handbag. It's a text message from her flatmate, Tia: u hme late? indn takwy gud? Faey is punching in her reply when out of the corner of her eye she sees a woman heading towards her stall. She quickly turns, so that her back is to the entrance, and waits for the precise moment when she knows the woman is about to enter, before saying, her back still turned, 'Welcome.'

As intended, the woman is startled and impressed.

Faey turns around and smiles a warm, welcoming smile. 'Please come in and take a seat.'

The woman enters and sits down. She says nothing at first, just looks about her.

Faey seizes the opportunity to make a quick assessment: the woman is alone, no friend in tow. So, a falling out, perhaps? Or is it no lover? Dark rings under the woman's eyes suggest sleepless nights. Faey notes the Chloe handbag and Manolo Blahnik shoes – no money worries, then. She detects the cat hairs clinging to the woman's overcoat: a beloved pet at home. Time is up, the woman is watching her, but there's enough for Faey to get on with.

'Let's start with names, shall we? I'm Faey.'

'I'm Jennifer.'

'Okay, Jennifer. All you need to do is sit back and relax. I'll do a few preliminary things to get us underway. Soon I'll start to pick up on things. As these come through I'll relay them to you, and you just let me know when I'm on the button. Whatever you need to know will unfold like a vision, a story. It's as simple as that, really.'

'Okay.'

'Any questions?'

'I don't think so.'

'Good, then let's begin.' Faey gazes searchingly into Jennifer's eyes, before shuffling and cutting her stack of spirit cards. She slides the top card off and sets it face down before her with her right hand resting over it. Then she closes her eyes and takes in a slow deep breath through her nose. As she exhales, her chest drops and she whispers an enigmatic incantation, a construct of her own invented language that creates an air of mystery with her clients, and makes her appear to slip more fully into the role of psychic:

Ca nu, ca nobleh nu, eh passu mon nobleh. Ci teh rond a nu, feteh a cincum bo. Ester nu. Ester nu. Ester do.

She opens her eyes slowly. Then she goes for it: 'What is the name of your cat?'

The woman is surprised. 'My cat? Oh! Mr Moggles.'

Faey smiles. 'I sense Mr Moggles is a real comfort to you right now.'

The woman looks down and says, 'Yes, yes he is.'

Faey sighs. 'Animals are so often there for us when people aren't. They don't let us down.' She watches Jennifer carefully. Something telltale is bound to emerge soon. Sure enough, the woman's eyes well up. Ah-ha – tears are not far away. Always a good sign.

'I sense a hurt, Jennifer. Who would hurt you so badly?'

The woman sobs. It's the kind of gooey, lip-trembling flutter that can spell one thing only. Faey sends it out: 'I see a man. It's a man isn't it, Jennifer?'

Jennifer nods.

Faey continues, playing the best odds. 'He wants you to still be friends?'

Jennifer scrabbles in her bag for a hanky. As she blows her nose she mumbles through the material, 'He walked out on me.'

Faey takes a punt: 'Forgive me for this, Jennifer, but the sex, it hasn't been right for a long time, has it?'

Jennifer lets out a sad, tiny yelp and nods.

Faey looks on her with compassion and cranks up the intimacy; it's time to cement their sisterhood: 'Oh, Jen – can I call you "Jen"? – Jen, you're thinking it's because of *you*. That *you* weren't good enough. Couldn't satisfy his needs.'

The woman's eyes harden and she crushes the hanky into her tight fist. Good, thinks Faey, anger is so much easier to work with. She now feels safe to push on into unknown territory – it's all in how you handle it. 'But he was a bit, how should I say this …?' Come on, come on …

'Kinky!' blurts the woman.

Oh! Well … okay, go with that.

'Let's just say his needs extended to the unusual, shall we?' says Faey, still probing.

'But Jen, Jen! You are above all that!'

Jennifer says, 'He insisted I urinate on him when we had sex.'

'Golden showers,' says Faey, sighing.

The woman nods, shamefaced.

Faey smiles, and just can't help herself: 'Well it's a piss-poor show, if you ask me!'

For a moment Jennifer stares at Faey, and then in an instant they both dissolve into guffaws of laughter.

Great! The turning point – every session has its turning

point, and this one has come early. Now Faey is confident she knows what this woman needs. Because all of the assessing, the guessing, that goes on in her sessions is really about Faey finding out what her clients need. This is how Faey sees her job: helping people to feel better about their lives when they leave than they did when they walked in. Social work with a psychic spin, she tells her few select confidantes.

And Faey is clear she is not meddling. Take Jennifer, for example: the fact is she herself made the decision to come and see a psychic, which shows she's ready to move on, needs to put the pain of a troubling and broken relationship behind her. Faey is simply facilitating Jennifer's life journey. Healers, she is quick to point out, work in many different ways.

Now for the close, the all-important summary – time to lay it all out so the punter will go away thinking it was Faey and Faey alone who gleaned everything about her, saw her like no other, understood her like no other, and – joy of joys – opened her up to a bright new future.

'Jen, you don't need me to tell you this but I will anyway. You are a desirable, attractive woman living a life many would die for. You're successful, and you surround yourself with beauty.' This stands to reason – she's got the dosh.

Faey continues: 'You've been on a journey of the heart that's had many twists in the road you've travelled. You knew the path had somehow veered off into brambles and bracken, didn't you, Jen? Cutting you, hurting you!

'But you were strong, so strong – and so committed – that you stayed the course, even though you knew it was growing dark and you were in danger of getting lost.

'Until your man …' Faey pauses expectantly.

'Maynard,' says Jennifer.

Maynard? Wow, Faey certainly hadn't seen that one coming!

'Yes, Maynard – he took the left fork and headed off alone, hoping that he might find some way to satisfy his tawdry yearnings.' Faey likes the metaphor. She stretches it: 'While you, Jen – the strength of you! – have kept on course. You see, you've taken the *right* fork … towards the light.'

Faey leans forward earnestly. 'I see that light, Jen. It surrounds you. It radiates from you. You don't know it, but you are basking in its glow right now.'

Jennifer is openly crying now, tears streaming down her cheeks.

Faey smiles, 'And best of all, Jen – best of all – you have dear, loyal Mr Moggles to remind you what love is all about, until the real thing comes along.'

And finally, just to make sure hope is kept alive and not swallowed by doubt or despair, Faey pauses, closes her eyes, and says: 'For I see another in your future, Jen. Yes, another man, a good man. A loving man worthy of you! And I see your heart opening like a rose, full in flower and scented like Heaven.' What a great line to end on!

As luck would have it, the music on Faey's tape player finishes just as she utters these momentous last words. She quickly reaches down and clicks it off before the next track kicks in and spoils the magic. What a show! She's earnt every penny of her twenty-five quid and then some.

Just one more act for the finale: Faey reaches out and takes one of the woman's hands in hers, and says, 'Jen, shall we look at your spirit card now?'

Jennifer nods, and Faey slowly turns the card over.

Bingo! It depicts a medieval princess lifted high by tiny putti with fluttering wings, escaping the stone-arched window of a tower so high it sits in the clouds. The princess's eyes are closed; there is a beatific smile on her face. Couldn't be better!

Faey smiles and says, 'Well, there you go.'

The woman gazes at the card and shakes her head in amazement. 'My friend came to you a few weeks back,' she says.

Faey is on a roll. She does a quick mental inventory of recent punters, assessing who might be the match: who would live in the same moneyed area and be of similar age, who would be most likely to share the story of her own session with Jennifer? Got it! Two weekends ago – her name was Sharon.

'Sharon,' says Faey, matter-of-factly.

'That's *right*!' says Jennifer, her eyes widening. 'Sharon said you were good. But I had no idea. You're *amazing*! Thank you, thank you so, so much!' And she reaches in her bag for her purse, pulls out three ten-pound notes, and says, 'Please keep the change.'

Faey takes the money and says humbly, 'The gift of my gift is that it might be a gift to others.'

As the woman departs, Faey says, 'Goodbye, Jen – may all the graces smile over your every step.' Adding: 'Do feel free to pass my name on to your friends. Remember: Faey by name, fey by nature.' Because let's face it, there's no better advertising than word-of-mouth.

The day may have started late, but it's a steady one. Faey talks a teenage girl through the loss of her first job, a middle-aged housewife through an ongoing and nasty dispute with her neighbours over their endless noisy renovations, and finally a young couple desperate to conceive their first child after two years of trying.

Faey is about to start blowing out candles when she becomes aware of a man standing before her stall. She calls out to him: 'Hi, there! I was just thinking about shutting up shop, but I won't yet, since you're here for a reading.' The fact that he's standing there and not entering gives her a pretty clear lead, so she goes for it. She pops her head out through the doorway, smiles and says: 'I know you're feeling a bit unsure – but we both know you've come this far and have no intention of not following through with it.'

She has hit it on the head. He smiles briefly and walks into her space. 'Please sit down,' says Faey, indicating the chair. She's already started her study of the man, noticing the slight limp as he moves. Is he getting over an injury? He's well dressed, in a studied, casual manner. His hair is neatly cropped. Probably a professional. A lawyer maybe? Or a banker? Perhaps in the financial markets? He's not big, but is well built – probably works out. She can smell something subtly sharp and tangy under his after shave ... what is it? Got it – chlorine! He's been swimming.

She begins: 'Let's start with names, shall we? I'm Faey.'
'I'm Alan.'

'Okay, Alan. Just sit back and relax. What I'll do is look at you for awhile. Then I'll draw a card from the stack. Soon I'll start to pick up on things. I'll just say what I'm getting, and you let me know when anything resonates with you. Whatever you need to know will emerge. That's really all there is to it – so any questions?'

'Just one: are you an Aussie or a Kiwi?'

Faey smiles. 'Kiwi. Anything else?'

'No,' says Alan. 'That's all.'

'Good, then let's begin.' Faey shuffles and cuts her cards, selects one, puts it face down on the table, then closes her eyes and recites her mantra. She slowly opens her eyes and looks into Alan's.

Play it safe to start: 'You're happy in your work, you're successful. No money worries. In fact, I see lots of money.'

'Not all mine, I'm afraid,' says Alan.

'But you handle a lot of money.'

'Yes, I'm a stock-broker.'

Bingo. 'You try hard to look after yourself. Your body, I mean.'

'Yeah. I go to the gym, but not so much lately.'

Faey chances it: 'Since the accident?' She sees the surprise register in his eyes.

'That's right! Came off my motorbike a few weeks ago. I've been having physio.'

'Well, that swimming's certainly a good idea.' Again Faey sees Alan startle. 'Keep it up. Low-impact exercise will do that leg a world of good.' She sees he is impressed.

She continues: 'But we both know that's not why you're here.'

Alan gazes at length into Faey's eyes. 'No,' he says, finally.

Faey fishes: 'I sense a loss.' There is so often some form of loss.

She sees the tiny wince, the hurt creep into his eyes as they soften with sadness. Boy, she's on form today. She tosses the line out again: 'There is a youthful energy around you.' She watches carefully.

Alan looks down, and out it starts to come: 'You mean *was* around me.'

She plumbs for it. 'A child.'

Alan nods.

Now, a fifty-fifty call: 'Your son?'

'Daughter.'

'But the name I'm getting, it could be a boy's?'

'Yeah, I guess so, depending on how you say it. Dominique.'

'Ah. Dominique, Dominic – I was a bit confused.' Good recovery.

Now, what kind of loss? Faey's mind races. Marriage split maybe? Something more serious? Ill health? Death? She probes on.

'Alan, this hurts you. To talk about it, I mean.'

'Well, no-one likes to admit failure, do they?' says Alan.

'Certainly not. But you're perfectly safe here.'

Alan smiles sadly. 'When Sarah walked out on me, I thought I could cope. Things weren't right for a long time, so I figured it was the best thing for both of us. I just never counted on how it would feel to not have Dominique in my life – you know, daily. Seeing her grow, talking about what she did at school, watching her play.' His eyes moisten. 'I miss all of that so much!'

Alan's words burn deep into Faey. Briefly, unavoidably, she revisits her own parents' break-up, the acute childhood pain of it. How terribly she missed her father, especially when a few years later he remarried and shifted to Oz and the phone calls and letters dwindled. She still carries the loss, muted though it may be, like a secret, poorly healed wound – scar tissue, hidden from all but herself.

Faey forgets the pretence of foreknowledge. 'Oh, Alan. Are they far away?'

'They're in Edinburgh now. That's where the new fellow lives.'

'That's harsh,' says Faey.

She needs to say things, needs to soothe this man, give him hope. For Dominique's sake. She needs for him to not give up on Dominique.

Faey is looking at Alan, sitting with his shoulders slumped, when there is a blinding, blurring flash of colour, a sudden smearing of the room around her – and in an instant it is she herself who she is now watching. Faey is seeing herself from Alan's side of the table, through Alan's eyes. She watches the Faey opposite stand up and, as money is handed over, bend down briefly. She sees her wave goodbye. Now she is walking up the passage as the market is closing around her. She pauses to look in a window, then enters one of the shops. She emerges, and glancing down, sees a big, soft teddy-bear under her arm. Now she is exiting the tunnel. Crossing the canal. She is in the pressing crowd as it stumbles its way back towards the underground, packed tight and barely shuffling. So she steps out into the High Street to bypass the thick of it. There is a horn blast, the screech of tyres. Faey sees a blue and white sky tumble past her eyes. Then nothing.

'You okay?'

Faey slowly becomes aware of the session again, again feels her weight upon the chair. The candle on the table swims back into focus. Looking up, she sees Alan watching her, a worried expression on his face. 'You alright?' he says. 'Can you hear me?'

Faey shudders, takes a deep breath and smiles shakily. What the hell was that? Did she fall asleep? Have a crazy dream? Some kind of weird out-of-body experience? Whatever it was, it's a first.

She is shaken, and feels slightly nauseous. Should she mention it to Alan? But then Faey decides to get back to the business at hand: for the one thing she *is* certain of right now is that she can't let anything get in the way of her really helping Alan and Dominique in their time of need. It's her overriding duty to look after their best interests – help fix a dreadful wrong. Like her own past, their very futures are at stake.

'I was just, er, tuning into your finer vibrations, that sort of thing. Now, where were we?'

'Edinburgh,' says Alan.

'Ah, yes.' Faey collects herself. 'Look Alan, you're a successful man, a really nice guy. And you're a loving father. The kind of man, the good male role model, that Dominique so needs in her life.'

She looks at him imploringly and continues: 'You might be considering whether to move to Scotland to be nearer to Dominique. Or maybe you don't want that because of your work or whatever, so you're wondering how to keep up a meaningful relationship with your daughter from here in London: how to manage regular visits – you going to see her, and Dominique coming to stay with you. But in a sense, Alan, none of that matters. It's just nitty-gritty detail and something a man of your capabilities and strength can definitely sort out.'

Faey sighs. 'The thing is this, Alan, without you in her life Dominique will grow up wounded. And the same holds true for you. What I hear from Spirit right now is the need for you to undertake, profoundly, to never give up on Dominique. Never turn your back. Never disappear. Even when it hurts. Can you do that, Alan? Can you swear to stand by your daughter, now, and always?'

Alan sees the earnestness in Faey – feels the power of her conviction. 'Yeah,' he says, 'I swear. I mean, of course I do. I owe her that. Anything less would be wrong.'

Faey feels a huge sense of relief. She smiles. 'Oh, Alan. So mote it be. So mote it be!'

Alan stands and smiles. 'Well, I guess that's that. Thanks a lot. It's been helpful. What I really needed to hear right now.'

Faey smiles back brightly. She feels something inside her has shifted, she feels lighter.

'Twenty-five pounds, right?'

Faey nods and rises as Alan hands over the cash. One of the banknote slips from his hand and flutters across to Faey's feet, and she stoops to scoop it up. Straightening up again, she watches as Alan walks away. He momentarily stops, turns around and waves. Faey, feeling a warm glow inside, returns the gesture. She calls out, 'Do feel free to pass my name on to your friends.'

Doors are shutting, lights are switching off, flattened boxes and bags of rubbish are being stacked in front of various stall fronts. Alan notices a big, cuddly purple teddy-bear in the window of a shop that is still open. It's Dominique's favourite colour. On impulse he enters.

Faey goes to blow out the big red candle at the centre of the table. Then she sees Alan's soul card still lying there unturned, forgotten in all her urgency and determination to steer Alan towards the future path she so clearly understood he needed to follow. She swings around and pokes her head out of the doorway, hoping to call him back, but he's disappeared from view. Faye turns back to the card and flips it over. It depicts a man, a medieval knight in a suit of armour. He is hanging upside-down, dangling by one foot from a spindly branch sticking out the side of a high cliff-face, perilously near the top. Far below on a ground strewn with jagged rocks lie his helmet, slipped from his head, and his fallen sword.

Alan exits the market and squeezes onto the busy

footpath. It's mobbed with hundreds of tired end-of-day shoppers, all shuffling towards the tube. The throng creeps along at a snail's pace.

To bypass the thick of it, he steps off the curb, out onto the road.

Out onto busy Camden High Street.

THE PARK

A SMALL HEAD appeared from behind the trunk of an aging birch. Sharp, beady eyes carefully appraised their surroundings. Minutes passed in complete stillness before the sandy-grey body emerged fully in a single bound. Now in open view, it froze yet again on the lawn, tail held high and poised, ever ready for flight. Soft green grass concealed its tiny arms and legs. More minutes slid by. Then a second unheard all-clear must have sounded, and the squirrel executed four more quick leaps, only to again pause and stand sentry.

'Hello, little friend,' I said. 'Joining in with the weekend crowds?'

No answer came back, but then what was I expecting? I stretched my legs out, leaned back on my elbows and shifted my gaze skyward. A puff of wind lifted a jiggling kite into view. I watched it climb into an overcast sky that set a soft light dancing over the busy lake.

Around me crowds of people ebbed and flowed. The elderly shuffled. Mothers ran to intercept children bolting to the water's edge. Teenagers milled aimlessly, eyes glued to their phones, or chattered in self-absorbed clusters. Joggers jogged, strollers strolled, lovers loved. Families gathered in ragtag groups.

I watched as the kite dipped then rose again on its line, responding to the delighted tugs of a tiny giggling blonde child. She was dressed à la Kensington, and stood not five metres from where I lay sipping plastic-encased water supposedly from somewhere pure and untouched in Wales. I thought to speak to her but she was so beautifully focused on her play that I left her to her reverie. I looked back to my furry four-legged companion, but it was now nowhere to be seen.

Lying fully on my back, I lifted my chin until my eyes viewed the surrounds upside-down. This inverse world, framed in green at the top, with people hanging by their feet over argent clouds, made me think about how we see. Or, rather, about how what we see is informed by how we choose to frame it. I thought back to the paintings I'd viewed just a couple of hours earlier in the art gallery which bore the same name as the nearby water, currently teeming with an armada of pedal boats: The Serpentine.

I had wandered into the cool of the gallery as respite from the crowded park. I'd not heard of the exhibiting artist, Artyom Chernavin, a Georgian whose entire body of work came out of the 1970s. Not a happy chappy, apparently: he killed himself in 1979, at the age of thirty, on the same day the Russian army confidently strode into Afghanistan. Chernavin's oeuvre, said the leaflet accompanying the exhibition, reflected his interest in some arcane branch of the occult.

I found his paintings compelling: abstract planes of colour intersected by blurs of realism, hints of the figurative dissolving into the coloured flatness. So subtle were the glimpses of the sad-faced beings inhabiting this shadow world that I had the impression of only just managing to catch them at the very edge of their existence; that unless I snatched my head in a precise, peripheral moment, I'd miss all signs of them and they'd simply vanish. The effect was both dreamlike and disturbing.

'That your child?'

A voice snapped me back to the present, and my world tumbled right way up. In front of me stood a forty-something man walking an enormous black Rottweiler. I looked over to the girl with the kite, then back to the stranger. He wore a faded U2 t-shirt, sport shorts, running shoes and a tan. Fit, no doubt from the endless walks the heavy-headed, slobbering beast at his side demanded. He nodded to his left, not at the girl but to where I now saw a small pushchair. Its back was to us both, but we could glimpse, just over the top, the head of what appeared to be a very young child. I looked back at the man and shook my head. I stood up, and both of us moved to where we could see the front of the chair. Its occupant was a baby doll, startlingly lifelike.

'Looked real to me,' said the dog walker with a shrug, as he and his massive charge turned and headed off towards Knightsbridge.

I gazed at the doppelganger. Of course it wasn't alive. Yet its fabric body slumped in that way common to certain types of padding: not so much a collapse as a gentle exhalation, a sighing fold. Viewed from behind, the softly tilting body looked totally lifelike.

'Me, too,' I agreed, but he'd already gone.

Looking back at the doll, my mind returned to its earlier contemplations. Is the nature of reality, I wondered, defined solely by the vantage point from which it is viewed? Chernavin seemed able to come to terms with this, on canvas at least. Though, given his dénouement, maybe he didn't come to terms with it at all.

I turned and wandered along the lawn's border towards the water's concrete shoreline, with its fussing sergeant-major geese and preening swan princesses. Head down, I followed my grassy trail gently around to the left into yet more crowds. Above the babble of varied accents and languages, I detected a different sound: a gentle but insistent medley of hissing, chattering and finger snapping. I allowed the movement of the masses to guide me through an open gateway to where I eventually looked up to see the sound's source: the rush and tumble of water in the Diana, Princess of Wales, Memorial Fountain.

I made my way to the edge of the rippling concourse, a wide and shallow channel draped expansively over gently rising lawns to form a large and lazy oval. Contemplative clusters of people meandered around its perimeter, tracing curves that were not regular but defined by the varied elevations of the landscape. The shape appeared almost heart-like. Not the sweet, stylised symmetry of a valentine heart, ordered and predictable. No, here was much more the outline of a true human heart, full and round for part of its journey, flat and straight for another: the uneven mapping of something natural and unruly. From the fountain's highest point at the top of the heart, the water welled up from its subterranean source to flow out in two opposite directions.

How very like the late princess herself, I thought: torn between royal duty, on the one hand, with all the stifling sham it represented, and the insatiable yearning of a spirit to be free and self-determining. No surprise that the water, in its tumbling travels down each of the heart's sides, bucked, frolicked and jolted; until reaching the bottom, where the two flows rejoined, lulled in a brief interlude of peace and calm before being invisibly sucked into the earth and drawn up to the top to face the music all over again. I couldn't help but smile at the appropriateness of the metaphor.

Then, out of the corner of my right eye I noticed something move. The dancing kite. I looked up and watched it jiggle and jostle. On its colourful red surface I could just make out a hint of decoration: a naïvely drawn face, presumably painted by the child herself. Close-set starry eyes and a lopsided mouth surveyed the scene below. The same gust of wind that now ruffled my hair swung the kite around so that the painted face's gaze fell directly on to me. The face somehow looked familiar. I'd seen something like it before. But where? How did I know that face? Those eyes?

The Serpentine Gallery! The kite's face looked like the macabre photograph of Chernavin printed in the exhibition flyer. He was dressed in a black hooded cape, holding an upturned skull with a flaming candle stuck on it. Now I could see, despite the childishness of the kite's artwork, the strangely strong resemblance.

As I studied the kite, pain suddenly seared through me, as if my body were tearing in two. I gasped as it coiled in my chest, like a burning hand grasping deep into my flesh and jerking me towards it. At that moment, my soul was wrenched from my body. Down below me, I could see my abandoned form lying on the grass next to the fountain, torso twisted, legs splayed, arms askew. As I watched on, passers-by began noticing my prone form, some approaching, others simply standing and gawking.

Then, in one swift swinging swoop, I found myself facing west, looking out towards the massive red-brick roundness of the Royal Albert Hall, and across the road from it the garish gold-and-marble monument to its royal progenitor and namesake. I pitched and fluttered as a series of small, sudden tugs began. I felt myself being drawn inexorably forwards and downwards, lurch by lurch. Victoria's consort drifted out of view behind the tops of trees, and soon all I could see was the small blonde child looking up at me, drawing me to her, reeling me in like a trophy trout. As she wound me down, one hand over another, her eyes bore into me. Eyes that were not those of a child.

With a bump I found myself held fast in her tight, tiny grip. But this was no sweet innocent. I could see now that this was Artyom Chernavin himself!

'My God,' my thoughts screamed, 'what's happening to me?'

He leaned forward and peered at me, framed by a halo of blonde curls. 'Gotcha!'

'I don't understand! This makes no sense!'

'Yes, it does. I've caught you – and now you are mine.'

'But how?' I protested, utterly bewildered. 'Why?'

He grinned. 'Because I can.'

He leaned even closer and whispered at me in his girl-child voice: 'Because I have the power. The secret.'

'What secret?'

He looked around, before saying, almost nonchalantly: 'To life everlasting, of course.'

I shuddered.

'I am a reaper,' he explained. 'I reap bodies in which to dwell.' At this, he erupted in a chilling girlish giggle.

'But … why *me?*'

'You looked. You stared. I saw you wonder.'

He continued after a pause. 'You see, I read. I studied ancient texts. Then I practised. Oh, you've no idea how long I practised. And, at last … the breakthrough!'

'You're crazy! This is crazy! I mean nothing to you. You're a madman!'

He snapped back: 'Ah, but I should be a *dead* madman, should I not? Yet here I am … alive.'

'Look, please. I don't understand any of this. This is insane!'

He ignored me. 'The breakthrough, you understand, was in the paintings. They were the missing key! Not just any paintings, of course: they had to be self-portraits.'

My soul cried out to weep, but my tissue paper eyes remained dry and staring.

A sinister smile crept over his face: 'Do you know how many I've travelled within since my passing? Seventeen! Can you imagine that? Seventeen different men and women! Oh, and now … a child.'

His eyes clouded over. 'But never again a child. No, never again. Too risky. I cannot afford to lose artistic merit.'

He looked at me. 'I must hold their eyes, you see. Long enough to make the leap, or I am lost.'

He held his small free hand up before his eyes, rotating and studying it. 'How can these young, unskilled, unworthy hands ever hope to capture the magic of my talent? The talent of my magic! No matter how perfect my inner vision, if I am incapable, too clumsy, too backward to bring it out …'

His eyes flashed: 'You saw my efforts this time. Dismal!'

He waggled his fingers: 'Ugly, damned, useless little things! How I hated producing so risible a face. Can you imagine my shame? Barely able to make the sloppiest schoolroom scribble!'

'Please,' I begged. 'Please let me go.'

His tone became matter-of-fact: 'Oh, no, no, no. But trust me, with my brilliance and your body, together we'll make great things. And when it's again time to move on, when we come to paint the facsimile of our face, it will once again be a laudable effort!'

A roaring sound filled my ears, so I could barely make out his final words. I felt my body squeezed like it was compressing into itself, and then everything drifted into darkness.

'It's okay, you're okay. Don't worry.' I found myself looking up into a sea of faces. Nearest to me, kneeling over me and looking concerned, was a middle-aged man. He was Indian or Pakistani.

'Wha-what happened to me?' I mumbled. 'Where am I?'

'You're in Hyde Park. I'm a doctor. You've had a collapse. I saw you fall, but you've come round now. Just lie still for a bit. You'll be alright.'

Post script

It has been three weeks since I had my strange turn in Hyde Park. I am pleased to report I've had no further fainting spells. I've come to realise that the nightmarish dreamscape I found myself in while I was out to it was no more than my fevered mind's delusional distortion of parts of my afternoon's wanderings: the strange art exhibition, the young girl with her kite, the babbling of the fountain.

My life goes on the same as before. Same job, same flat, same girlfriend. In my spare time, however, I've taken up a hobby: I've started painting. And, if I do say so myself, I've caught on rather quickly.

THE UNDERGROUND

THERE I WAS heading south on the Northern Line, pulling into Angel shortly before five-thirty on a Friday evening, just one of the commuting sardines packed tight into our rattling tin cans, when I glanced down at my frowning watch face. *You're late, mate,* it said. As an afterthought, it added: *The late, great Ken Lacrosse.* Brilliant, I thought, watch wit! A tisking Tissot! Eleven- and one-o'clock Roman numeral eyes glowered at me. *Wouldn't want to be in your shoes, Kenny boy* — its voice rising as I let go of the passenger strap I was hanging onto and tugged down my parka sleeve — *when you get home to the missus!* From under the fabric, I could just detect a muffled: *Your goose is cooked!*

Now there are times when late means an annoying little delay with irritating repercussions. Dinner going cold on the table, kissing goodbye to the start of a movie, no time for airport duty-free indulgences. Those shit-oh-well-that's-life moments. Then there are times like now, when you've sworn to your wife that come hell or high water, in spite of your past occasional (never to be forgotten!) parental lapses, there is simply, absolutely, positively no way on earth you will be late for your daughter Julia's junior school orchestra recital tonight.

Not after all Lizzie's motherly dedication and endless patience supporting your daughter's daily practices and weekly lessons, theory studies, bowing technique, 3:4 time and semi-quavers. Not after her loyally listening to every brain-squeezing squeak and squawk you yourself have mostly managed to avoid (missed out on, says Lizzie) due to your working hours.

No way you will ever break *this* particular promise, and along with it (according to Lizzie) Julia's young and fragile heart. While in the process, it goes without saying, piss your wife off throughout all eternity. My tetchy timepiece was absolutely right, I was in for it!

I felt bad, of course, bloody awful. I did a quick mental calculation: at best, by the time I'd changed at Bank, dashed over to Monument, hopped the Circle Line to South Kensington, then raced down Harrington, around the corner into Queens Gate and on to St. Augustine's Church where the recital was being held, I'd have missed a good three-quarters of the performance. Oh, Christ!

The train lurched to a stop and the doors opened to another determined, crushing crowd, surging in and out of the aisleway where I was standing. That's when I first saw him, glimpsed him through the brace of stiffened backs, the forest of raised arms, the blur of faces, all with their carefully averted underground eyes. What a sight! The kind of person you look at and know immediately they must be as eccentric as all hell. He was wearing layers of shabby jumpers that jumbled and poked about. His outermost garment was a loose-knit thing, the colour of week-old offal. This was tucked under the waistband of a pair of plaid plus-fours, far too large for his frame but held up by paisley braces. Below the pants dangled alarmingly skinny legs, which instead of being clad in knee-high stockings, were left rough and raw down to mismatched ankle-socks: one blue, the other traffic-cone orange. The brogues on his feet were black and beaten. My eyes made their way back up to his face. It was old and craggy, cheeks and chin peppered with grey. Tufts of white hair poked out from under a faded leather cap worn back-to-front. He sat mumbling to himself, occasionally looking up to squint eyes at the other passengers. He was comical, shocking and sad, all at once.

I was about to look away when his eyes locked onto mine. I quickly averted my gaze, but after a while I couldn't resist peeking back at him under the guise of looking in his general vicinity. His eyes were still glued to me. I looked down at my feet. The air was hot and stuffy, and I felt a trickle of sweat running down from under my raised arm.

Halfway between Moorgate and Bank the train slowed to a standstill and the fluorescent lights fluttered into darkness. A groan rose from the carriage. After a few moments the lights came back on, and the tinny, disembodied voice of minor officialdom crackled through the encased overhead speakers: Ladies and gentlemen, we apologise for this delay, which is caused by a signal failure up ahead. We will be underway again as soon as possible.

A murmur rippled through the car. I glanced over again towards the old man, but he was gone. How anyone could move in that packed rail-car was beyond me. I leaned my head from side to side, peering around the blockade of human cargo. He couldn't have just disappeared.

'Be off again in no time,' came a voice from behind me, thin as tissue paper. I turned and nearly jumped out of my skin. He was standing right next to me, eyeballing me like before.

'I-I-I- …' I stammered.

'Cat got your tongue?' he said.

I scrambled for composure: 'I … er, didn't expect … I mean, you were over … How'd you manage to get over here?'

'Not that there'd be enough room to swing it.'

'Sorry?'

'The cat – not enough room to swing a cat.'

He smiled to himself. Then he looked about.

'We'll be up and running before you know it.'

And, like a prophecy, a shudder and thrum of engines ran through the train, and we slowly began to move forward.

'Funny old girls,' he mused. 'They've certainly earned their stripes.'

'You like the tube, then?' I asked.

'Keeps this city on the map. Take away the underground and all you have is a giant town with no way for folk to get around. Lose the underground and you lose London's greatness, plain and simple as that.'

'I never really thought of it like that.'

We approached Bank, and he said: 'Most escalators.'

I looked at him.

'Bank. Coming up. It's got the most escalators. Fifteen of them, plus two moving walkways.'

'I didn't know that,' I said.

'But Angel has the longest one. One hundred and ninety-seven feet long. Vertical rise of ninety feet. Longest in all of Western Europe.'

'You know a lot about escalators.'

He laughed. 'Shortest one's at Chancery Lane. Only rises fifteen feet.'

'Fifteen feet, huh?' I decided to humour him. 'That's not much.'

'Four hundred and nine of them – in total.'

'Escalators?' I asked.

'Altogether they travel the equivalent of two trips around the world,' his eyes sparkled. 'Every single week!'

'My,' I said, at a loss for words.

'Sixty-four lifts.'

'Lifts is it now?' I smiled, somewhat indulgently.

'Know where the deepest one is?'

'Ah, no, I can't say I do.'

'Hampstead. One hundred and eighty-one feet straight down into the earth.'

We pulled into Bank.

'Well,' I said, 'I'm getting off here.'

'Most platforms,' he said. 'Bank.'

He nodded in the general direction of the platform.

'Actually, Bank and Monument. And Baker Street. They all have ten.'

'I see. Well, thanks. And, ah, cheerio.' I wasn't sure why I was thanking him. I squeezed out the doors with the mob.

Remembering Lizzie and Julia, my heart sank as I dashed as best I could through the crowd. Riding up the escalators I recalled that Bank had the most of them. And platforms. How handy: tube trivia – my life at dinner parties was forever transformed!

I made it onto the Circle Line, heading west towards South Ken, again standing cheek-by-jowl in the squeeze.

'Ever think about the pumps?'

I snapped around to find the same eyes searching my face. 'You again!' Startled, my raised voice broke the tacit mores of underground etiquette. Feeling the silent reproach of those around me, I continued under my breath: 'H-How'd you do that? You following me or something?' I tried to make it a friendly inquiry, but I couldn't hide the accusatory tone.

'Oh, I just ride. Something for an old man to do.' He smiled at me. 'Seven hundred of them.'

'Seven hundred of what?' I asked.

'Drainage pumps. Just think of that – seven hundred. In over four hundred sites. Pumping away, faithfully keeping us from getting our feet wet. After all, we're often under sea level.'

'I guess we are.'

'Just south of Waterloo is the lowest point below sea level. Seventy feet.'

'You certainly know a lot about the underground.'

'Respect it, I do. Two hundred and eighty-seven stations, twelve different lines, two hundred and forty-three miles of routes. You've got to respect that.'

He looked around him. 'And we had the first,' he continued proudly. 'The Metropolitan. Opened January 10, 1863. First underground in the world.'

'That is something,' I agreed.

'Two hundred and eighty-seven stations and only twenty-nine of them south of the Thames.'

'Ah.'

'Know how much of it's in tunnels?'

'South of the Thames?'

'No, the whole system.'

'No, I—'

'Forty-two percent.'

'Goodness,' I said, genuinely impressed.

'A mighty amount of tunnels,' he proclaimed.

'It's a lot alright.'

'Longest continuous tunnel? Northern Line, East Finchley all the way to Morden via Bank: seventeen-point-four miles of tunnel.'

'Really? A seventeen-mile tunnel?'

He looked me straight in the eyes: 'So what's bothering you? You're a right old fidgety-britches.' I was as disconcerted by the abrupt change of subject as I was by his sudden interest in me.

'If you must know, I'm running late for an extremely important date. I'm supposed to be at my daughter's school orchestra recital at six. I promised I'd be there on time.' As I spoke I realised just how great the sense of shame was that I was feeling. I couldn't make light of this one, not this time. I knew in my heart I'd failed both Lizzie and Julia.

He regarded me closely, thinking for a moment. 'You sure about that time?'

'Of course, I'm sure. I even put it in my phone. I just forgot to check it, even once, over the day.' I felt like a shit a thousand times over.

'Seems to me if I were organising an evening school concert, I'd make it seven at the earliest. Not six. Not at dinnertime. Got to allow for parents like you needing to get there from their jobs, and for the kids to have a meal. You can't expect them to play on an empty stomach.'

I looked at him. He shook his head and said, 'I'd check that time now if I were you.'

A glimmer of hope pulsed through me as I fumbled for my phone. I scrolled through my calendar and there it was – *Julia, 7pm, St Augustine's*.

'My God, you're right – I have the time wrong!' I laughed hysterically. 'Oh Christ, what a relief!' My joyous outburst drew glares from my fellow commuters. Contrite, I whispered, 'Thank you. Thank you so much! How did you know?'

He smiled. 'Common sense. Besides, you can't be a headmaster for twenty-eight years without knowing something about how to plan these sorts of things.'

How did an ex-headmaster end up like this? I wondered. 'Really? You were a headmaster? Fancy that. Well, I'm so relieved – you wouldn't believe it!'

'This one's one of the shortest, you know.'

'Sorry?'

'The Circle. Only thirteen miles long.'

'Er, no, I didn't …'

'Of course the shortest line is very short. A smidgeon. Waterloo and City, just one-point-four miles.'

Ah, I thought, lucidity gone.

'Know the longest line?'

'I'll take a stab … Picadilly?'

He looked at me with delight. 'Close, very close! Picadilly's number two. Just one-point-six miles less than Central. Central's forty-six miles long, you know.'

'Well, there you are.'

'How about the busiest station?'

'King's Cross St. Pancras?'

He shook his head. 'No, that's number three. We're coming into the busiest one right now.'

I looked out the window. On the walls I could see the signs: Victoria.

'Over eighty-six million passengers a year. Imagine all those people.'

I tried to picture eighty-six million people. It was impossible

'And that's just one station! You'll be getting off soon.'

'That's right – South Kensington.'

His expression darkened. He looked away and whispered under his breath: 'Victoria, and Kings Cross St. Pancras.' Then he seemed to snap out of it and resumed the role of statistician. 'Victoria, and Kings Cross St. Pancras. They both have the highest number of one-unders each year.'

'Sorry?'

'One-unders.'

'What are one-unders?'

'Suicides.' He looked at me. 'In New York they call them "track pizzas".' We both smiled and he shook his head: 'Americans.'

We pulled in and out of Sloane Square. I noticed the wistful look creep back into his face. 'Eleven a.m.,' he said.

By now I knew to wait for the fuller explanation. It was some time in coming.

'The most popular time for them,' he finally mumbled, staring distractedly into the middle distance.

The train began slowing down. I bent down to retrieve my briefcase from between my legs. 'Well,' I said, straightening up, 'it's been really interesting talking with—' But he was gone.

I looked left and right, then again, and again. I even squatted and checked among the legs around me in case he'd collapsed to the floor. Again, I drew scowls from those around.

Pulling into South Ken, I joined the flow from the rail-car. I skipped up the short flight of steps, then stopped at the top to check my watch. Its face stared back at me blankly, no hint of its former agitation. Not only was I on time, I even had a quarter of an hour to spare. With the relief came another thought, and I made my way to the ticket window.

'Is the station manager in?'

The bored-looking assistant turned in his seat and shouted something into the back of the room. He told me to step around to the side door. After a few moments it opened to reveal a rotund middle-aged man with a pasty face. His blue uniform gave him an officious appearance, but he turned out to be interested and helpful.

'I'm wondering if you could help me?' I began. 'Would you know of a passenger …' and I went on to describe the old fellow. The manager began nodding as soon as I mentioned the plus-fours.

'Sounds like old Wentworth. Keen on facts and figures about the underground?'

'I'll say!'

'Always traveling the lines. Guess it's one way to spend your retirement.'

'He was like a walking textbook,' I said.

'Oh yes. A bit of a legend really.'

'Is that all he does, just lives on the underground?'

'He's under ground alright,' the station manager chuckled. 'Dead since, oh, I don't know, "98 – or was it "99?'

'What do you mean?'

'I mean what I say. He's dead.'

'But I was just talking to him … on the tube … we spent some forty minutes together.'

'Yeah? And who was sittin' across from ya – Elvis?' He laughed at his wit.

'No, really, I'm serious. He can't be dead! We talked about escalators … and pumps … and the lengths of the lines.'

'That's Wentworth, sure enough. But I'm tellin' ya, mate, he's long dead. Died the way he wanted to, I guess you'd say.'

My mouth was dry. I felt the hairs on my neck prickle.

'How did he die?'

'One-under. Eleven a.m. Victoria Station. Not a pretty site, by all accounts. You okay?' the manager asked. 'You look ill. Wanna sit down or something?'

I shook my head.

'It's the busiest, you know,' I finally managed.

'What is?'

'Victoria. It's the busiest.'

THE HEATH

THE FIRST TIME I flew was no easy thing. I'm not talking about airliners here: no Boeings or Airbuses, or for that matter those smaller Cessna kind of things. No helicopters, micro-lights, or paragliding. No hot-air balloons. And – just so you don't thing I'm being clever – no trippy drugs either. No, I'm talking about the real thing, actually lifting both feet off the ground and simply moving through the air. Except 'simply' doesn't describe it at all. There was nothing simple about it.

I was alone in my home. It was the middle of the night and I'd just woken up and shuffled off to the loo for a pee. I live by myself – one failed marriage, when I was too young to know better, had been more than enough for me. These days, in my mid-forties, I'm a happy longtime convert to the many desirable liberties of bachelorhood.

So I was heading along the hallway, yawning my way back towards the bedroom, naked, because that's how I sleep. I'll never understand how anyone can expect a good night's kip when they clothe their body in fabric and then lie between two more layers of fabric, and all night long everything clutches and grabs at you. A total violation of your freedom of movement. Freedom of movement – that's what you get when you fly. Complete and utter freedom of movement. Except when it's your first time!

You might be wondering, since I'd never flown like this before, why I would even think to attempt such an outrageous thing? All I can say is I suddenly knew with all my being that I could – and I had to get on with it right then and there, in that very moment. It's actually like this every time. I can never just decide on a whim to take off. Rather, it comes over me. I'm suddenly aware flight is upon me, and if I just yield to the knowing, off I can go.

So overwhelmingly compelling was this urge, the first time, that my mind didn't even go to the place of thinking I had no understanding whatsoever about how to actually go about it. But looking back, I realise I must have had some notion, some kind of innate, instinctual knowing of what to do. Like a baby bird, I guess. And just like a baby bird, I had everything to learn!

Standing there in the hallway, I just held my arms out in front of me and leaned forward a little bit, like I was on the edge of a swimming pool all set to dive in. Then I lifted my left leg and held it out behind me, standing on one leg wobbling. Briefly, I became conscious of my mass, of the weight of me bearing down on my one foot. I felt the softness of the carpet beneath it.

The moment of truth – I carefully lifted my other leg. The instant my right foot was off the ground I rocked violently from left to right. It was ridiculous how unbalanced I was, how unsure of my own centre of gravity. I didn't place my foot back down, though, but nor could I raise it any higher. I just remained there suspended, body more or less horizontal, right leg dangling just off the floor.

I continued rocking and jerking back and forth, immersed in the newness of the sensation. Imagine lying on your stomach, stretched out like Superman, on a thin, tautly stretched piece of rope that runs under the entire length of your body. Imagine how unstable you would feel, falling first to one side and then to the other, always rolling, grappling, trying to somehow pinpoint that elusive stable centre-point. It calls for hyper-vigilance and a need to anticipate: a constant micro-adjustment of weight-shifts determined in nano-seconds. It took me a good ten minutes to gain even a modicum of control.

And that was only the most immediately difficult bit.

As I slowly raised my right leg ever higher, not only did the ungainly rolling increase again, but I also realised, in the struggle to keep my body straight and parallel to the ground, my stomach and back muscles were tensing to the point of rigidity. I may have had gravity on the back foot, but in no way was it letting go entirely. In fact, it never really does. Even now, as I confidently swoop and soar, I am ever-respectful of that force of nature which, given half a chance, would snatch me without a moment's notice and hurl me back to earth.

It's nothing like floating in water, which at least has some viscosity to help keep you buoyant. With flying you are in the air, in a virtually frictionless space offering you no support whatsoever. My diaphragm ached. Invisible knives sliced into my lower back. I shook and shuddered, straining not to fold into an inverted V.

This was when I became aware of the next tricky thing I needed to master: how to keep from pitching up and down like some sort of manic seesaw. One moment my body was pointing up towards the ceiling, and the next my head was just off the ground. The knack, I discovered over the course of another tumultuous ten minutes, is counterintuitive. You have to to relax. Which was the absolute furthest thing from my reeling mind and tormented muscles. But thankfully, as I continued to gain the upper hand on the rolling, I began to loosen up. Enough to reduce the dizzying extremes of the pitching motion and maintain at least some approximation of horizontal control.

So there I was, not flying, but most certainly floating in the air. A sense of exhilaration pulsed through me. This was really happening!

For the first time I allowed myself to look around, and take in the hallway from my new floating vantage point. I was about a metre off the ground. When I turned my head to the left I saw the small oak hall table tucked against the wall. In the gloom I could just make out the ghostly white of the paper nautilus shell with its implausibly delicate frills. And next to it, the equally white piece of flat, chalky North Dakota hillside, cleaved to reveal its secret interior: the fossilised remains of a Paleolithic fish, its rust-coloured framework like a schematic etching of some Victorian metalwork fancy. I remember in that moment thinking about evolution, about the weird and wonderful workings of nature over aeons of time. Was I to be one of a new breed of human? Was this our race's next step: was our destiny to take to the skies? My lapse in concentration immediately had me pitching and rolling again, till I refocused and steadied myself.

Yet further refinement was required. I needed to figure out how to overcome the yawing. For no apparent reason I would suddenly start to rotate sideways, to the left or the right, like a dangling mobile. I squirmed and shimmied as I attempted to correct these back and forth swings. I tried opening out my arms and legs, only to discover that as soon as I moved them from my 'flight position' I would begin sinking to the ground. Clearly this would prove useful when it came to landing, but at this point I was nowhere near ready to come back to earth. Luckily, being in the hallway, the walls on either side were near enough that I was able to push off with my fingers whenever I came into contact with them and propel myself back towards the centre. This went on for some time. Had I been in the middle of a bigger space I might have bobbled around in circles endlessly. I gradually got a feel for it, learning to counter and control the swings with the slightest of rolling actions.

It all links together, you see. No one motion occurs in isolation. Instinctively, I brought to mind the image of seagulls hovering on the wind. At first they appear motionless, but if you look closely you see they are constantly making hundreds of tiny corrections, the silent whirring of a thousand lighter-than-air spindles and sprockets, a network of invisible linkages: the capricious clockwork of flight.

By this time, in spite of the breakthroughs and

exhilaration, I was becoming exhausted. Sweat from the continuous physical and mental strain was running into my eyes, causing me to blink wildly. Still I continued. I wanted more.

The problem now was how to get any forward motion. Since remaining aloft meant my legs had to stay together stretched out behind me, I couldn't use them to thrust off the walls. Kicking as if using a paddleboard in a pool proved ineffectual and I again began to drop. So there I remained, bobbing and flexing, like some naked suspended larva.

What I had yet to realise was that while roll, pitch and yaw are all embedded in the real science of flight – the actual physics of it – propulsion itself is dependent on something far more mysterious and metaphysical: intention. The incredible power of thought, driven by nothing more than absolute desire.

It turns out that to fly, fully and freely, one needs to give oneself over completely to the omnipotence of purpose and passion – the will – and its inexplicable effects on a world otherwise made up of, let's face it, mere matter. It was only when I wanted to move forward more than anything else in the world, needed to with every fibre of my being, and my surrender to longing was total, that I began to silently drift forward.

Oh the sensation! No feeling of being pushed or dragged along by some tangible force, just a slipping through the air. My breath caught in my lungs. I could just make out my wide eyes and crazy grin reflected back at me as I bore down on the wall mirror at the end of the hallway.

But now was no time for another lapse in concentration. At the fast-approaching end of the hallway an opening on the right leads into the adjoining passageway. To make the turn, I instinctively tried rolling and yawing slightly, and to my astonishment I successfully flew around the corner. That's right: *flew*. No doubt about it, this, at last, was flying!

I continued gently flying down the next length of passageway, gliding past my bedroom on the left, before negotiating another right-handed turn at the end to find myself now floating into the kitchen. I was still at my starting elevation, at about the same height as the bench I was gliding alongside, past the espresso machine, the microwave, the hob and oven. I slipped silently by the toaster, just glimpsing my body bending and distorting in the stainless-steel corners like a fun-house mirror. Then past the sink, the evening's unwashed dishes stacked in the bottom.

I moved through into the dining room, where my body floated over the table – barely. At the height I was flying I was only just clearing it and behind me I heard the shuffle and rustle of a few unopened envelopes from the day's mail catching on my feet and dragging along the wooden surface.

I clearly needed to gain elevation. To do this would require pitch. As I exited the dining room and entered into the lounge, I realised I'd arrived at the perfect testing ground.

My home is in London: Highgate, on the eastern side of the rolling green hills and vales of Hampstead Heath. The dwelling is large, staid and comfortable, and from the road appears like any of the other houses on the street. Strict heritage codes forbid me making any alterations to the exterior, so it looks virtually unchanged from when it was first built in 1865.

But inside I've made a number of dramatic changes. The kitchen, dining and lounge areas have all been ripped out and rebuilt. The lounge is large and has been opened out in height and extended into some of the far passageways, in doing so casting off much of the fussiness of its Victorian heritage.

I like the room's masculinity. It has white oak parquet flooring set off with rugs from Turkey and Morocco, a handsome selection of spot-lit objets d'art and paintings, a large wall-mounted screen with projector, and in one corner, a mirror-and-glass 1920s art deco bar complete with original stools and lighting. By taking out the floors immediately above, the room reaches up two-and-a-half storeys, overlooked by a wide mezzanine opening closed off with curved wrought-iron railings at the very end of the upstairs passageway. Here I had some ten metres of vertical space, thirty metres of length and twenty of width to play around in.

Now was time to test my elevation theory. As I floated towards the black leather sofa, I flexed and arched backwards, pointing my outstretched body upward by some fifteen degrees. Sure enough, I sailed gently skyward. I aimed myself even higher and found myself heading towards one of the ceiling corners.

Then I took what turned out to be a premature risk and willed myself to increase in speed. I shot ahead, covering some five metres in just moments! In a panic I thought 'slow down', but the sight of the looming wall and ceiling clouded my concentration and I crashed into the corner, shuddering violently as I scraped along the ceiling edge's decorative cornice at alarming speed. In a few seconds I'd covered the width of the room, banged to the left around the corner and was now careening along its length. I slammed into the next corner and again continued on my bruising way. Thankfully, after the initial shock I was able to focus my intent fully on slowing down and almost instantly I was cruising once again at a controlled pace.

I soon got the hang of flying gently in wide circles around the room's perimeter. And I learned I could drop in elevation by either aiming downwards, or easing my arms and legs out of flight position to sink horizontally, like a Harrier jump jet.

After a while, though, some internal voice told me clearly and unequivocally that my flying time was over for now. Indeed, that would become the pattern: the urge – and with it the ability – to fly always disappears as suddenly and mysteriously as it arrives.

I levelled out, slowed to a hover and, opening out my legs, allowed myself to sink to the ground without mishap. After more than an hour in the air, I could barely walk. Legs trembling, I collapsed into an armchair, both elated and exhausted. Eventually I managed to stagger my way back to bed, and in spite of my back's agony and my body's aching, cramping stiffness, I fell into the deepest of sleeps.

And that was it – the first time I flew.

As I said, it wasn't easy.

But I have since become a very good flyer. Now, whenever the knowing descends upon me, I take to the air like I was born to it. For some reason I can only fly unclothed. Which makes sense if you think about it: I mean, how could a bird fly in pants? Or a bat in a jumper?

Obviously I can't allow myself to be seen flying, and not just for reasons of modesty. Nothing would be more life destroying than becoming some sort of celebrity flying freak. Fodder for the paparazzi and the target of endless tabloid scrutiny. Or, even scarier, the subject of government scientific study and experimentation. No, my secret remains with me.

But on occasion, after dark on warm nights, I succumb to temptation and slip outside to escape into the night sky over the Heath. I buzz the cream-coloured spire atop nearby St Anne's Church, swooping rapturously around its fine golden cross, before setting a north-west course out over the patchwork of reedy, bush-clad bathing ponds. I circle the broad, gentle tree-ridged rise of Parliament Hill and meander the skyways over scrubby woodland and winding walkways, the twinkling city lights below encircling the blackness of my playground like some fantastical fairy ring.

I take care to never venture further than the Heath, or stay out longer than an hour, just in case my flying reverie should suddenly depart and leave me stranded in, let's face it, rather awkward circumstances. But while I'm airborne, well, there's nothing like it on earth! Little joke.

And I'm getting more daring. In the safety of my lounge I'm starting to teach myself acrobatic manoeuvres. Flips and rolls, stalls, that kind of thing. I guess I'm a stunt pilot at heart.

I realise I may never know whether this is my own unique and precious gift, or if given the chance people everywhere could learn to fly. But such freedom, such boundless freedom!

To record and preserve my experience for posterity, just in case anything should ever happen to me, I've written it all down here – the full story, faithfully documented. Everything has occurred exactly as I've stated. I cannot emphasise this point enough: this is a true record of fact. It is not – pardon the pun – some fanciful flight of fantasy.

Michael L. Challis,
11 February, 2016.

'So what do we do with it?'

'Stick it in the file with the case notes for the coroner. Let's face it, the guy was some kind of nutter.'

'Pretty weird though, don't you think? I mean after what he wrote. Broken neck and him lying here starkers and all.'

'Took a fall, plain and simple. I'd say he tumbled over that mezzanine railing up there. It's a big drop. Probably drunk – or maybe on drugs. Could've even topped himself.'

'Still, you gotta wonder.'

'All I've got to wonder about is getting home to tea. Forensic's shot through. The photographer's finished up. Let's get the ambulance guys in to bag him and get the hell out of here. It's the coroner's baby now.'

THE GARDEN

AS DUSK FALLS he is poised in street-bound stillness amid the hurly-burly of Christmas crowds. In the winter chill he stands, a counterpoint to the surrounding visual cacophony of shouting signs, shimmering shop windows and cascading fairy lights. He is the Blue Man and he offers a brief and easy entertainment – a semicolon for passing homebound workers and snap-happy tourists.

Against the flashy backdrop of Maxwell's Restaurant he has set up shop, balanced atop his blue-painted wooden box, blue cloth spread out over the cobbles before him, a small silver dish resting central upon it containing a decent scattering of coins. As the seething Covent Garden throng ebbs and flows past him along the gentle rise of James Street, the Blue Man stands steady as a meticulously carved lapis lazuli boulder.

He is dressed in the garb of a mid-eighteenth-century gentleman, a single-toned blue gentleman from head to toe. His coiffured blue wig sits handsomely above the frilled neck of his blue shirt and his coat's high collar. His ponytail, complete with blue bow, hangs down the back of his blue tailcoat. A blue waistcoat tops blue breeches, which end just below the knee, meeting long blue socks that dive deep into heavy-buckled blue footwear. His elegantly expressive hands are clad in blue gloves. Only the whiteness of his staring eyes, rimmed with the faintest peek of red, offer the warming hint of a beating human heart.

So captivated are his ever-changing audiences that they forget this is a Blue Man at work. They don't see parked behind him his scruffy carry-all, empty now of costume and props, and packed down with faded Levi's, Converse shoes, sweat shirt and worn duffel coat. For here is a career effigy: a blue other-century jobbing statue – a Blue Man who has learned the secret art of standing still, forever entranced, day into night warding off blinks, backache and boredom. So do look, stay a moment, because when someone drops a coin before him, he'll burst briefly into life. Just watch.

A young woman, splintering off from her group of friends, is poised to toss her twenty-pence coin on the pile. She peers intently at the Blue Man's eyes, which are fixed over her head on the bored youth opposite selling hot roasted chestnuts.

Clink, rings the silver dish …

Instantly the Blue Man responds to the sound. His eyes return the gaze of his attractive young benefactor. He notes her impossibly long lashes, and beneath them her warm-grey eyes. In a slow mechanized flourish, his right hand drops from his chest to align with his waist. His left arm rotates from his side to slip in behind his back. With the suggested whir of secret sprockets and spinning cogs he nudges slowly forward into a long and elegant bow. His head respectfully dips, and as it does his entire torso stretches so far out front of the vertical that surely he will spill, tumble, topple from his perch. But no, his shoes, invisibly anchored to the box, outfox expectation. The mannerist manoeuvre is sheer grace and beauty, and brings with it a delighted gasp from the dark-haired beauty. Then, in a practice-perfect final flourish, the Blue Man reaches his right arm forward, palm opened outwards, fingers raised artfully, and gently presses against – nothing. He pushes himself off of invisible air and fully retracts in a mirror reversal of the entire clockwork movement. His automaton eyes release the young woman back to her friends, and he again looks into the distance, locked in his frozen pillar pose.

He sits straddling a large spherical rock perched at the water's edge. Tepid waves wash over his feet. His back is burning under the tropical sun, but he doesn't move. He is entranced by the sunlight's diamond dance on the fluid surface. He narrows his gaze through the blurring filter of his lashes, the sunbursts making him think of all the stars in the Milky Way going supernova at once, smearing across a shimmering sky. He feels so light, so insubstantial, that he fears if he averts his stare even for a moment from the water's lightshow he will rise and be lost like a wafting, wandering balloon.

Her hand comes to his rescue, resting on the small of his back. So hot is his skin, and hers, that her fingers seem to singe in parallel bands.

'You are far away, no?' And indeed he is, so far away, so unable to unglue his eyes from the glimmer, that it takes some time for him to whisper, 'Oh yes.'

She reaches her other hand around his front and teasingly tucks her fingertips under his waistband. 'I wonder can I

*bring you back? Or are you lost forever?' He hears the smile
in her voice, its suggestive undertow. His sun-addled brain
is slow to function – he listens to himself repeat the question
internally. He drags forth an answer: 'Lost forever? No … I
don't think so.'*

*'Mmmmmmm,' she utters, and her nails wiggle further
down into the Lycra cavern. Deep within he feels a rippling
rush, insistent in its surge. He smiles and mumbles, 'I'm coming
back.' 'I know you are,' she whispers in his ear.*

*He stands over her naked body as it lies sideways across their
unmade bed. Her long dark hair is damp from the shower and
clings to her shoulders like seaweed. It is their first holiday to
Thailand, to the palm-covered island of Koh Samui – a break
long overdue, a welcome escape from London's December chill.
Her body lies stretched out and slightly rotated, languid and
titillating like a Modigliani nude. The soft underside of her
arm is exposed as she shields her eyes from the midday glare
glancing over her body through the doors opening onto their
outside deck. He looks down at her small brown nipples, at the
little shadows they cast over the goose-flesh surround of her tiny
puffed breasts. He delicately places his hands over the swells, feels
the stiffening against the inside of his palm. It is a proposal, a
request – and she responds by rolling so that she lies fully flat
on the white sheets. Almost inperceptibly she arches her hips,
slowly, so slowly, until the searching sunlight tumbles onto her
lifting mound and tangled triangle. 'Bonjour, Mademoiselle,'
he says. 'Bonjour, Monsieur,' she replies huskily. Her eyes slowly
open and she looks longingly into his. He feels himself growing,
nodding upwards. Her gaze shifts. 'Oh, Monsieur,' she says*

and she reaches her hand forward. 'I think I can maybe be of some help, no?'

Clink … The Blue Man performs for a small boy of four or five, who backs uncertainly against his father's legs and turns his head into the trousers' brown fabric.

Clink … An elderly woman smiles and reaches out her own arm to comfortingly pat the back of the Blue Man's fully extended hand.

Clink … A sneering teenager, showing off to his mates, mocks and mimics the Blue Man but loses interest when he finds he cannot penetrate the performer's world.

Clink …

The Blue Man's stare locks onto eyes so intensely blue they rival his own costume. He is aware, peripherally, of the swath of red hair dancing above them like marsh fire. He silently thrills to the lilting Irish voice.

Her skin is white — so white against the nighttime oily darkness of the Grand Canal that she seems to glow with a half-life of a thousand years. She raises the wine glass to her mouth and he watches the red liquid meld with her painted lips. She looks radiant. And she knows it. The Rialto Bridge, packed as ever with its mass of pointing tourists, rises to the right of their waterside trattoria. Vaporetti chug pass, as do water taxis with their throaty diesel throb, tossing in their wake the bouncing black arabesques of gondolas. On her forehead he notices the slightest beading of sweat on this muggy night.

'I love Venice,' she exclaims in her lovely singsong way. 'Its

crumbling union with the sea. All the wear and tear, the decay. It makes it seem even more romantic, don't you think?' It's a rhetorical question and he knows he need not reply. Every time she excitedly turns her head in a new direction to catch the ever-changing scene around them, he thrills.

'I love you,' he finally says, and she looks towards him with her dreamy eyes and smiles. He shrugs in surrender, and says it again: 'I just love you.'

They meander the back streets and canals, making random turns and allowing themselves to get thoroughly, hopelessly lost amongst the dim labyrinthine waterways. The crowds thin. Disembodied voices bounce under bridges, whisper around corners, and soon die out altogether. Eventually they come to the watery edge of a dead-end passage where they are completely, utterly alone. She kicks off her shoes and sighs at the relief the coolness of the flagstones gives her weary feet. She stands with her back to him, facing the jet black of the canal.

'Thank you,' she says, without turning. 'For this.' 'Oh, it is soooo much my pleasure,' he replies, and he embraces her from behind. She giggles and tisks gently as his fingers begin unbuttoning the front of her dress. She allows the material to drape open from shoulder to shoulder. He eases her bra upwards until her full white breasts, visible even in the dark, rest against her ribcage. Then, cupping a hand beneath each, he softly lifts them, just enough to feel their weight. It is so beautiful he wants to cry.

Clink … A blanket-wrapped old man, shrinking into his wheelchair, laughs aloud as his middle-aged daughter points him towards the Blue Man: 'Well done, well done!' he manages, in a thin, wispy voice.

Clink … A small girl looks up at the Blue Man with the studied stare of a scientist, standing so close that he almost grazes the top of her head when he bows.

Clink … 'Quick, George, you gotta come and see this!' shouts a short, stout, scarf-strangled woman in oversized pink and white running shoes, her Texas twang so sharp the Blue Man winces inside.

Clink …

Her eyes are impossibly amber, the colour of wild bush honey or the finest tanned leather. Bordered above by a short, tightly braided bed of wiry black moss, and below by the most pronounced bronze-blushed cheekbones he's ever seen. Her full lips smile and part in pink and umber perfection.

At six feet tall, her statuesque frame was born to be adorned, and the clothes she wears look as if they were built directly upon her. He loves walking beside her towering figure, watching the inevitable snap of heads, male and female. For such a sight is the thing of catwalks, not here amongst the wafting steam and touting, shouting seafood stallholders selling fresh-cooked shrimp, scarlet-shocked lobsters, stuffed crabs and oysters on the shell. Making their way through the Fisherman's Wharf crowds, as the late morning sun peaks proud of the Bay's blanket of fog, one charmed purveyor reaches out and gifts her a cardboard cup of bisque, and she laughs a thank-you before breathing deeply of the briny brew.

They face empty Alcatraz, wander out to where the piers extend their wood and concrete fingers into the harbour's chilly waters. Suddenly she runs ahead, not releasing his hand so that he must stumble along at her same loping pace, arm outstretched and tugging. When at last she stops she is panting. She winds him into her. In a rich brown voice she says in his ear: 'S.F. Now this is my kinda town.' And laughs. Then she trains her glowing eyes on his and adds, 'And you, mister, are my kinda guy.'

In the middle of the night in their hotel room in Union Street, long after the clanging streetcars have ceased their up-and-downhill rumbling, he awakens. Something has disturbed his sleep. He lies still and listens intently in the dark. Then he hears it again. She is talking in her sleep. The words themselves are incoherent, but the inflections are urgent and carry a sense of alarm. He wonders whether to wake her or not, but then she lifts herself up on one elbow and sleepily says, 'What?' Startled, he replies: 'What what?' 'What do you want?' she asks. 'Nothing,' he says. 'You were talking in your sleep.' 'Was I? What was I saying?' 'Couldn't tell, sorry.' Their eyes adjust to the night's half-light. He sees the outline of her long arm as she lifts it to scratch the top of her head. 'I'm wide awake now.' 'Me, too,' he replies. She remains sitting, he lying, in a long, silent tableau. Just when he thinks he is falling asleep again he feels her take his hand. She slowly lifts it to her mouth and sucks on his fingers. Then she lowers it and moves them between her legs. She hunches over him and he feels the bounce of her breasts on his chest, as her lips seek out his, followed by her searching tongue.

Clink … A trio of Polish men in cheap leather jackets stand resolutely in front of the Blue Man, leaning slightly on one another, their arms crossed in silent anticipation of the show.

Clink … Cameras flash en masse as a school of Japanese tourists bid the Blue Man goodbye and swim off into the night's cold current.

Clink …

Turquoise-green. Can that be a real colour for eyes? he wonders. He is riveted. It is the blue-green of old Silk Road jewellery hanging heavy in silver-embellished clusters. It is the outrageous colour of cleverly concocted cocktails, stuffed with floating fruits and tiny umbrellas. It is the sandy sun-drenched shallows of reef-ringed South Pacific shores. That's it – he knows exactly where he'll take her.

They stroll hand in hand, sending up soft clouds of straw-coloured sand with every lift of their feet. Her long hair, the same colour as the sand, floats on a sighing warm breeze. A sailboat tacks in the distance, its fluttering sail punctuating the air in brief staccato applause. Her white muslin dress flaps, too, shot through with glimpses of the lavender two-piece beneath. They stop and share the softest of lingering kisses. When her eyes open she sees him staring deeply into them. 'The colour of Noosa,' he smiles, 'that's what they are.' She pulls a face. He continues, warming to the description: 'It's true, they're the exact aquamarine of these tidal estuaries. Somehow you have managed to inspire this land from the other side of the world.'

Their walk has taken them as far out as they can go on the spit. They are alone under a quivering Queensland sky – just the line of pines running down the length of beach behind them, the sun-baked sand and timeless swish of gentle waves. He feels his longing for her grow. He pulls her tight against him until she notices his need pushing beneath her navel. She squirms against his insistent thrust. In a sudden swoop he dips his head, and bites her nipple. She shrieks, wrenches herself free and slaps him full across the face. 'So that's the plan is it?' she shouts. He stands back in shock, rubbing his throbbing cheek. 'Wh-what was that about?' he manages. 'I could ask you the same. You presume way too much, mister!' 'I don't understand,' he pleads. 'You understand plenty! Just who do you think you are?' Her eyes flash with such anger they visibly darken – gone is the turquoise-green. 'Do you really believe you can do anything you want with me? That I'm just some sicko fantasy playmate of yours?' 'It's not like that – it's romantic …' he stammers, but she is screaming at him now: 'Mentally conjure up your dream setting, place me into it, and watch me put out? Creep!' She strides off down the beach. 'Control freak! Why don't you try the real world?' Her image wavers, begins to break up. Evening darkness and shuddering cold pour in from the edges. Endless summer melts away as everything folds in on itself. Still, he hears her one final indignity: 'Go fuck yourself for a change!'

In the wintry nightlight of Covent Garden, the Blue Man stands his blue, blue ground; the consummate professional upholding his unerring vigil. Passing crowds continue to gather, coins clink, faces smile, mobs move on. No one notices the single blue tear slipping soundlessly down the Blue Man's cheek.

THE MUSEUM

CHRONIC PAIN HAS a way of etching itself into the sufferer's face. It marks and sets one apart. Just one glimpse of Henry Cotterill's worn visage and people would take a step back. His forehead was grooved and scissored, his cheeks and nose a crisscross of hatched red veins. The once soft and full bottom lip, now tightly drawn and grim. Grey stubble sagged off his chin into the deep folds of his neck. None of it drew you close.

Yet for those who did pause to look past the ravages of age and pain, one feature would surprise and delight: the eyes. Striking duck-egg blue, and, after eighty-two years, only just beginning to fade. Intelligent eyes, retaining a spark still quick to burn.

'Know your way around?' A loud voice assaulted Henry's right ear.

He turned to discover a young man at his side, with short, up-brushed hair, his face as unmarked as Henry's was tattered. He was clad in the official red polo shirt of the assistant workforce populating the Natural History Museum, identity card dangling from a lanyard. Henry regarded his inquisitor: how could someone so young, with so little experience of life, possibly act as a custodian in this place, encapsulating such a vast sense of history, the very passing of time?

The incongruity heightened as the enthusiastic young man inserted himself between Henry and the silent, burnt umber bones of *Diplodocus carnegii*, interrupting Henry's contemplation of the exhibit's information panel. He already knew the story well: in 1905, the Scottish-American industrialist and dinosaur-enthusiast, Andrew Carnegie, gifted the museum this replica of the original skeleton which graced the Carnegie Museum in Pittsburg, U.S.A., after King Edward VII, during a visit to Carnegie's Scottish castle, heaped royal praise over a picture of it.

'You lost? Can I help you?' the guide persisted, even more loudly.

Henry winced, snapping back: 'I am not deaf, young man! But I will be if you open your mouth one more time!'

Not willing to chance it, Henry turned and made his way across the Hintze Hall floor, its expanse a scattering confetti of tiny black, white, yellow, grey and orange tiles. As varied as the course of nature itself, thought Henry. For all its overblown Victorian splendour, this was a place he held dear to his heart.

Henry could still remember his first visit as a nine-year-old, bounding ahead of his parents up the sweeping outside steps behind the wrought ironwork of Cromwell Road. His feet skipped and danced as he passed under the arched entranceway and into the ornate cream and grey edifice, with its stately towers, carved animal gargoyles and oh so many windows. It was 1932 and England was only just starting to take note of a wild-eyed fascist agitator making waves in

Germany. 'If ever there was a face that would stand clogging, it's that one!' pronounced his father.

As events transpired, Henry's father's words were more than a little prophetic. The printing works of Cotterill & Co., by appointment to His Majesty the King, occupying a full city block in Hackney, were flattened in the very first week of the Blitz. A fortnight later, while sheltering in an underground tunnel during another night-time bombing raid, his father suffered a massive heart attack and died in the arms of an Irish brickie, his last gaze taking in kindly eyes and a dirt-streaked face.

By this time Henry was sixteen, and he went to work selling newspapers – for printing ran in his blood – to support his mother, who slipped into a world of silent weeping and melancholy, before slipping out of life altogether within two years.

Now, Henry walked the length of *Diplodocus*, his progress slow and faulty. The wear and tear of years, and the long since redundant need for any sort of speed, kept his movement lumbering and ponderous: 'Not unlike you, my bony friend,' Henry said, as he stood under the skeleton's impossibly long neck, remembering the absolute awe he had felt as a boy when he'd first seen the beast.

'I used to believe I could build a tree-house in there,' he said, smiling as he gazed up at the enormous armature of the rib cage. He recalled his childhood fascination, from that first visit onwards, with everything connected to dinosaurs: the *Terrible Lizards*. He loved the musty and exotic air of adventure and discovery: the idea of digs, the slow, secret emerging of bones turned to stone, the full-bearded serious scientists, with their coterie of man-servants, faithfully toiling in the far-flung reaches of Africa, Asia and the Americas. He was to return to the museum again and again throughout his youth, so that as the museum's collection and quality of information grew, so did Henry. It wasn't until the looming clouds of war took precedence over everything else in the lives of every Briton that his boyhood love affair waned.

'You haven't changed a bit,' Henry observed aloud, adding with a chuckle: 'Just like me.'

Then he noticed the tail, how gracefully it swept through the air, upwards and outwards, snake-like, in a neat counterbalance to the lifting neck at the other end. Well, that is different, he thought. A change from earlier theories that held that the tail must have swept along the ground behind the mighty reptile. Modern biomechanics now said otherwise. Henry thought wryly: Who said you can't teach an old dinosaur new tricks, eh?

Out of nowhere a jostle of back-packed school children swam around Henry like reef fish, their teachers frantically calling for order. He noticed some of the children look at him and point, one of them saying something which caused the others to burst out laughing as they melded back into the flow.

He looked to where the throng had disappeared through a glass-and-timber doorway into the Darwin Wing. Beside it, a tall hanging banner proclaimed: *T. REX RETURNS!*

This is all new, Henry thought, and he felt a tingle of anticipation as he made his way into the Ronson Gallery. He'd only come in after all these years to track down *Diplodocus* and say farewell. He passed through the doorway and along the passage until he came to another of the hanging banners: on this one, the tiny mean red eye of *T. rex* seemed to be challenging him to turn left and enter. I accept your challenge, Henry thought, as he paused to catch his breath.

The first thing that struck him as he moved into the room was the extraordinary juxtaposition of old and new. Here in the darkened space, threading amongst all of the elaborate stone-and-tile Victorian architecture, the endlessly carved pillars featuring animals and foliage, ran a gleaming overhead metal gangway. It stretched the length of the room: struts, guys, stainless steel and halogens, a twenty-first century Meccano construction wending its way through Henry's time-honoured Church of Natural History. As his eyes adjusted to the dimness, he found his way to the stairs leading up onto the gangway. Pushing aside his body's reluctance to face the climb, he slowly preceded upwards, step by painful step.

Reaching the top, Henry found the rows of guiding floor lights running along either side of his feet disorienting, more disco than dinosaur. Gazing out to either side, again his eyes adjusted to the new light to reveal a multitude of skeletons. There were more here than he'd ever imagined; it was overwhelming. So many, he thought, where once there had been just you, *Diplodocus*.

He encountered *Massospondylus*, not much bigger than Jonty, the old Irish Setter that had been his faithful companion throughout the 1960s. There was *Allosaurus*, like *T. rex* but smaller, positioned as if running down its next meal. There was *Albertosaurus* and *Dromaeosaurus*; and *Stegosaurus*, with the striking swathe of upright plates running the length of its spine. There was *Gallimimus*, ostrich-like but twice as big. There was the ever-popular multi-horned *Triceratops*, and the small pack-hunters called *Veloceraptors*.

'I never knew!' whispered Henry. 'Look at all of you!' Suddenly, from nowhere, a force struck him so violently that it rammed the breath from his lungs and spun him fully round so that he nearly fell. 'Watch out, old man!' yelled the youth as he bounced off Henry and ran off, his laughing girlfriend in tow, a blur of baggy denim and exposed flesh. Henry gasped and gripped onto the shiny railing with both hands. Minutes passed before the daggers in his side subsided enough for him to continue on. He took tiny, measured steps as he shuffled down the darkened slope at the room's end, and around the corner.

T. rex!

This was Henry's first face-to-face encounter with animatronics. He inched forward, hand over hand, alongside what appeared to be the real thing: a living, breathing dinosaur! Small children backed into the legs of their parents, and cameras flashed, capturing smiling faces posed in front of the rumbling beast. Its subterranean purr was an ominous cross between a Siberian tiger and a Sherman tank.

The massive head swung to and fro, beady eyes scanning the crowd hungrily.

T. rex seemed to suck in the very air around itself, before lunging forward with an earth-shaking primeval scream. The tail, airborne like that of *Diplodocus*, swung in a slow-motion version of a cat's angry twitch. The all-but-useless tiny arms dangled over massive upright haunches the size of tree trunks, feet planted permanently in a fabricated fibreglass facsimile of a Jurassic forest floor, complete with bursts of dry-ice mist.

Henry stood mesmerised. 'Oh, you pretty thing,' he muttered. 'You wicked, wonderful, pretty, pretty thing!'

People moved on – so much more to see and do – only to be replaced by the next wave of onlookers, but Henry remained riveted for a good quarter of an hour as the programmed sequence played over and over. Finally, with one last look at the mighty clamping jaw, all teeth and terror, he left.

He emerged to find that his journey down the ramp past the lifelike beast had brought him back to floor level beneath the overhead steel walkway. All about him stood dinosaur displays flanked by large information panels. They transcribed a winding course back through the room to its entrance. Henry closed his eyes at the thought of the walk ahead. The day was taking its toll. He felt sore, tender and tired. 'Sore, tender and tired,' he said with a grimace. 'Sounds like the title of a bad country and western song.' Sad tunes with themes of loss, unrequited love and loneliness. They seldom had happy endings.

Henry felt his mood shifting, leaving behind the boyish exhilaration he had tapped into since his arrival. He made his way over to the nearest panel. It read: *During 160 million years of the dinosaur era the world around them was constantly changing.* Henry reflected on his own era, the countless changes that had occurred in the world since 1923.

The world of the dinosaur was quite different from the one we live in. Henry's world, the one he knew so well, was quite simply no more. It, like Henry himself, had been swept aside by a culture that valued youth over experience, wealth over wisdom, quantity over quality, computers over people. To be sure, marvellous inventions were exploding onto the scene almost daily, yet in this frantic surge of progress something vital had slipped away. He couldn't put his finger on what it was exactly, but he felt the loss deeply.

He moved on to an exhibit featuring three different fist-sized black castings of dinosaur teeth. *All meat-eating dinosaurs grew new teeth throughout their lives, replacing old ones as they became worn.* Henry ran his hands over the replicas, while at the same time running his tongue over his own false teeth. Now there's something evolution's let us down on, he thought wryly.

A video screen caught his attention. It featured a computerised animation demonstrating how dinosaurs walked. *Moving and eating are vital to the survival of an animal and the success of its species.* Henry's head slumped. He felt a heaviness drape over his heart, a sadness seep into his marrow. Life had cheated him; he'd never married, never had children. Look at me now, he thought. I can't move worth a damn, can hardly keep my food down. I'm the fatherless only-child of a father who himself was an only-child. The success of the Cotterill species ends right here.

He dragged himself further along. *Alligator or crocodile skin is probably the nearest modern equivalent to what a living dinosaur felt like.* Henry felt the hard bony sample. He slowly raised a hand to his face and ran his fingers over the tough scaly patches on each cheek. A single tear welled and burst its bank, splashing his cracked fingernails.

Fossil evidence shows how dinosaurs suffered broken bones, cancerous bone growth and arthritis. Many other diseases must also have afflicted them. The pain in his liver reared again, the internal knife, it jabbed, stabbed and sliced. As the specialist had predicted, things had worsened considerably these past weeks. Henry could sense the growth, its poison spreading, eating him alive from within. Just like *T. rex:* never resting, always devouring, destroying.

Henry's tears ran freely, salt stinging his chapped lips. He coughed and sputtered, held a handkerchief over his mouth. *Quite suddenly, 65 million years ago, all traces of dinosaurs disappear from the fossil record.* A groan, a constricted gurgle, emerged from deep within. He couldn't breathe. He stumbled to the exit and somehow hobbled his way out of the Darwin Wing.

Back in the central hall, another red shirt approached, but he waved it away. Waves pounded in his head, muffled sonic booms filled his ears. He took one look at *Diplodocus,* one final look … and in that instant the entire world shuddered and froze.

Henry gazed around. All of the people were stopped exactly where they stood: mid-step, mid-conversation, mid-photograph. No movement anywhere. Not a sound could be heard, even from outside the building. It was like a single frozen frame from a busy crowd scene in a movie.

Then, a slow, mighty creaking sound. It popped and cracked and echoed around the cavernous space. Henry turned to see the dinosaur's huge neck swinging his way in a slow sideways arc. He stared in disbelief. The straining continued until at last the giant empty eye-sockets in the skull looked directly at Henry. Then the jaw stretched – the sound of pulled rusty nails – and the mouth opened.

'Ah, Henry. I see you've come to say goodbye.'

Henry said nothing.

The beast continued: 'But you look sad. Don't be sad, Henry.'

Henry sighed. 'I'm dying, old friend.'

'Of course you are. Nothing lasts forever.'

'But I'm scared.'

'Scared of what, Henry?'

'The end, I guess. The end of things.'

'Things?'

'Well, me.'

'Ah, extinction.'

Henry smiled grimly. 'Yes, I suppose it is – extinction.'

'Henry, all things must pass.

'But who'll remember me when I'm gone?'

'Living isn't about being remembered. Living is about valuing every precious moment you've been granted, good and bad. You are not a species, Henry. You are an individual. Unique to this world. Think of your life – your wonderfully unique life.'

Henry did think. He thought back again to the delight he had felt when first coming to this place. He remembered his mother's soft laughter. His first bicycle, a red Raleigh. The first time his father gave him a sip of ale. He recalled playing football endlessly with his mates in Finsbury Park. His first kiss with Patricia Petrie. The incredible celebrations at the end of the war. How smart he'd looked in his first three-piece suit. His first car, an Austin in racing-car green. His promotion to regional distribution manager. He remembered dancing to Sinatra with Girlie Myers. Long weekend walks with his loving, faithful Jonty. The trip to New York, gazing in awe over Manhattan from atop the Empire State Building. Pork vindaloo at Veeraswamy's. The cruise to the Bahamas. His one-end victory in the Singles Final of the Southeast Championship in Senior Bowls. Cornish pasties and Bakewell tarts. The Sunday papers. His trip under the Channel to Paris. The *Times* cryptic crosswords. Night views over London from Hampstead Heath. Teasing the young nurses in the day hospital. That lovely first cup of tea every day. And more, so very much more.

He looked up at *Diplodocus*, his duck-egg-blue eyes sparkling, eighty-two years young.

'It's been a life alright!'

'But of course it has.'

'Maybe I *am* ready to go.'

'Welcome to the club, Henry.'

Sound poured in as people burst back into hurly-burly motion. Henry shuffled to the museum entrance. He considered looking back one more time, but didn't. Stepping through the double glass doors, out into the chill of a London autumn afternoon, he wrapped his scarf tighter around his neck. It seemed he always felt the cold these days. The flare-up in his liver was easing again, as slowly he made his way towards the bus stop.

THE PUB

THE QUEUE ALONG Victoria Embankment started forming as early as seven a.m. Half an hour later, as Walter exited Temple tube station to join directly onto the tail of the throng, the long riverside smudge of black and red jerseys already numbered in the hundreds. The air was charged with anticipation. Penetrating the excited shouts, predictions and bravado were the incessant ringing of mobile phones: friends, arms raised to indicate their precise location, trying desperately to track down late arrivals before the pub doors unlocked and the swell packed down inside.

In the general hubbub Walter stood quietly alone. No one was seeking him out. Shy Walter, they called him in the Tesco warehouse where he worked, where his silence always spoke louder than words and he was forever conspicuous by his inconspicuousness. Given his stammer, the primary reason for his intensely withdrawn nature, the title was an act of kindness. At school, where kindnesses tend to fly out the window like a fifty-metre punt, Walter had been known, ruthlessly and inevitably, as W-W-Walter. He had been endlessly harangued, harassed and hung out to dry. He learned to get by largely by shrinking into himself, perfecting the knack of becoming invisible. His survival demanded that he got very good at it.

But all that was in the past. Here, now, comfortable in his anonymity amongst the ever-growing, ever-loudening bands of loyal Lions and All Blacks supporters, Walter waited for the pub's doors to open. Which didn't mean he wasn't as thrilled as anyone around him at the prospect of the impending clash of titans. Walter had been a rugby-union doyen since the age of five, when his father and two older brothers first began explaining to him the intricacies of the sport. He grew to love everything about it: the unique blend of strategy, sporting prowess and finesse, married to undeniable brute strength and, at times, all the reckless thuggery of a schoolyard scrap. There was something raw yet noble about a rugby match — at times it was positively gladiatorial, especially at Test level. The crowds, even as they constantly bayed for blood, would invariably, in a show of grudging respect, acknowledge and applaud demonstrations of dynamic brilliance from the enemy side. And whatever the odds, the predictions, the totally bleeding apparent outcomes, rugby was a game of imponderables. The shape of the ball, its erratic bounce, ensured that nothing could ever be taken for granted.

Awarding Walter a full-grown height of 5'8", destiny had robbed him of any possibility of perfecting his own game. His shyness merely served to drive the nail into his rugby career coffin. In phys. ed. class his school peers had been determined not to select W-W-Walter Jackson to play on their side. Inevitably he was the last to be taken, and always by a side with enough numbers to keep him firmly planted on the sideline throughout. So Walter watched and learned. And over time what he lacked in on-the-field ability and experience, he more than made up for in his complete understanding of the game. His knowledge of the rules, tactics, teams and their histories, and current player profiles, was unsurpassed. His brothers – one now living in South Africa and the other in Australia – would be the first to attest to Walter's brilliance in this regard. As had his father until his death five years previously.

At precisely eight a.m, a fully-psyched management and staff at last opened the doors to the Walkabout, and carefully monitoring numbers, began to allow the crowd – now well over twice as large as when Walter had arrived – access into the television-lined arena: the next best thing to a seat in Jade Stadium on a dark and sleeting wintry June night in Christchurch, New Zealand.

The alarm went off at quarter past six. Alison Mooney heard it from the shower, buzzing away until it finally stopped. She submerged her face under the nozzle and let the warm stream run over her face and down her body. She'd been awake since five a.m, too excited to sleep again once her eyes had opened. Today was the big day! All the months of hype and speculation – years, if you took into account the belligerent attitude of the Kiwis following the dazzling British win in the 2003 Rugby World Cup – had come down to this one morning. Kick-off, ten past eight a.m.

Out of the shower, she dried herself off and wiped steam from the bathroom mirror. For a moment she stood and looked at her naked reflection, something she very rarely did.

It wasn't that she disliked her body, more that she'd grown indifferent to it. She knew she couldn't really complain about her weight, it was neither too much nor too little. She had enough of a bust to give her the necessary curves. And her hair was probably her single best feature: it sat attractively on her shoulders, full and wavy and bursting with auburn highlights. No, Alison knew only too well the weakness that let down her side.

She stared directly into her face, into her clear brown eyes. Then she allowed her gaze to sink to her cheeks and chin, to the surface scarred and pitted mercilessly after the ravages of teenage acne. She'd been cursed with a kind of gender-hopping oily skin, the type usually only reserved for the most unfortunate of growing boys. Moonface Mooney, the bully girls at school would call her. Or Tin-Pan Ali, because her face, they said, with its indentations and pockmarks, resembled a beaten-up old tin frying pan. Or another popular taunt: Baby-Cakes, after the way Alison had, for a short time, vainly tried to cake on enough foundation to smooth out her features. One thing about teenage girls, there was never a shortage of cruel wit. She combed back her wet hair, brushed her teeth, and left the room.

Alison fried an egg, buttered her toast and poured a glass of apple juice, and carried it all to her small kitchen table. Pushing aside the sports pages of three different newspapers, she found enough space to put down her breakfast and eat it. She thought of the impending game and felt a surge of excitement course through her. Somehow, during those painful school years of rejection and ridicule, she had got through it thanks to, of all things, rugby.

It had started in 1993, the year of the last Lions tour to New Zealand. Alison had been where she usually was, at home watching TV, when she'd chanced across the live coverage of the first Test match: an entertaining, close-run thing that the All Blacks just squeaked through 20–18. She didn't really understand the rules but she was always quick on the uptake and by the time the second Test came around and she saw the Lions level the series, she had discerned how the game worked. By the deciding third Test she knew enough about rugby to realise how badly the Lions had failed as they were blown off the turf by a clearly superior All Blacks unit.

Ever since that time Alison had become a closet fanatic. It didn't matter that she had no friends at school, that each day was another study in silent mental torture. She had the entire world of rugby to captivate her. She watched the steady ascendancy of Australia; and the decline of South Africa, who then turned all predictions on their heads by winning the '95 Rugby World Cup; the constantly changing fortunes of the New Zealanders, who being a nation of barely four million, always amazed her at how they competed so brilliantly on the world stage; the feisty French, so often a case of show over substance, but never, ever to be written off; and Britain, who had given the world the game, and most recently had dispatched all comers to take out the 2003 World Cup.

Alison knew her rugby all right. And she knew, on this morning, for the opening game of one of the sport's most occasional of great international contests, there was only one place she had to be: the Walkabout, Temple.

A staggering thirty-one colour TVs, hanging from muscular steel girders, encircled the interior. At the far end was a giant screen and projector. Tall tables and chairs dotted the room, and couches and coffee tables ran along the mezzanine level. Down one full length of the room was the bar, with taps that began pouring at twenty seconds past eight, and never stopped until well after the game had ended. A giant central skylight, covered by a grid, sent diffused lighting over the gathering glasses of English beers, bottles of New Zealand Steinlager, Stella Artois, lemon-stuffed Coronas and mini-kegs of Grolsch. The orange concrete ceiling sported two giant aluminium ventilation ducts – fat, winding worms of silver that somehow kept the air fresh and unclogged by the cigarette smoke. Ten full-sized Peavey speakers shouted out to the room, just managing to keep the pre-game banter of the commentators audible above the crowd's racket. Pockets of singing, chanting red sat in clusters, their cheeks and foreheads glowing beneath badly drawn lion effigies. But as the name would suggest, the Walkabout was an unashamedly 'downunder' establishment. The sea of black, with their forest of fern leaves emblazoned over hearts, shoulders draped in New Zealand flags, were by far the greater in number. Within ten minutes the place was full, doors closed, leaving outside at least a hundred disappointed latecomers.

Walter stood near the room's centre, facing the entrance doors and the kitchen serving-hatch, where hearty cooked English breakfasts appeared in an endless stream, to be whisked away and delivered to those canny enough to get their orders in immediately, while the table waiters could still move. He watched one of the many overhead banks of TVs, listening first to the Lions' team song, then the New Zealand national anthem. He claimed no particular allegiance, but if he were really pushed he'd have to admit that deep down his heart was riding with the tourists. After all, history was not on their side. Since 1931 there had been eight series, and only in 1971 had the Lions not left those far-flung southern shores a vanquished side. It was time they once again showed what they were made of.

Alison stood near the room's centre, facing the far end of the room, her back to the entrance. The bank of TVs before her showed the All Blacks gathering mid-pitch to hunker down and perform their signature Maori haka, a war chant that challenged the opposition to match their fury. A hush fell over the room as something primal momentarily captivated supporters from both sides. Alison felt the hairs on her neck rise. She knew by rights she should back the Lions, or at least remain neutral, but it was no use, she'd always loved the men in black: their rugged athleticism, their self-effacing demeanour yet unmatched self-belief, and their incredible ability to win time and time again.

The game kicked off with a roar on both sides of the planet that shook the pub's walls. Drama and controversy, so often co-conspirators in Test rugby, reared their heads in the very first minute as an unpunished All Blacks tackle, as dodgy as it was damaging, took the Lions skipper out of the game and the rest of the tour. Within no time the All Blacks had put a penalty over to be 3–0 up. The first forty minutes unfolded – and the Lions folded. They made little headway, repeatedly gave away the ball, lost lineout after lineout, and seemingly had no answer as to how to do things differently. By the half-time whistle they were down 11–0.

All around him Walter heard the usual midway blather of the triumphant and the disappointed: part analysis, part speculation, part wishful thinking. He already knew the game was lost. The dismal Christchurch weather played to the All Blacks' strengths. But more than this, the Lions coach, Sir Clive Woodward, had gambled the Test away by selecting players on the basis of experience rather than recent form. His touring party was bristling with exciting new talent, yet virtually none of them were out on the pitch.

Alison listened to the inane and increasingly drunken views of the supporters around her, who, by her reckoning, should simply shut their mouths and possibly be thought of as stupid, rather than open them and remove all doubt. Not that she minded differences of opinion, it was what following sport keenly was all about. She just couldn't abide pig-headed ignorance about what made rugby, and a winning side, tick. And there was a lot of it in evidence around her right now.

The second half simply delivered more of the same. The knockout blow came when an All Blacks build-up culminated in their captain charging up the centre of the field like the proverbial wounded bull, off-loading a pass to his left wing, who made a searing side-stepping run to the try line. In their wake, on the wet turf, lay half-a-dozen red jerseys who could have, and should have, made the tackles to arrest the move. The game ended in a resounding 21–3 victory for the New Zealanders. Around the room, cheers of delirium and delight went up from the waves of black, groans and curses from the rest. But all applauded, feeling sated, and knowing there were two more Tests to go, so anything could still happen. Within just a few minutes, where before there had been standing room only, the pub's population had dropped by three-quarters.

Walter remained where he had stood throughout the match, listening to the post-match commentary. Around him were tables stacked to the hilt with empty glasses and bottles. Staff busily began attacking the mess. As one of the crew struggled with a full and wobbling tray, a bottle fell at Walter's feet. He bent down to pick it up and felt his bottom bang into something.

Alison was watching the after-match TV interviews when she felt a sudden jolt that knocked her forward a step. She turned, her hand subconsciously rising to mask her face, and glared.

'S-s-s-s-s-s-s …' Walter began. '… s-s-s-s …'

Alison wasn't expecting a man to be standing there hissing at her.

'… s-s-s-sorry about th-th-th-th-th …'

Alison was tempted to say the word for him, but she bit her tongue. She could see the struggle on the man's face. His neck was strained, his lips pursed and his eyes tightly squeezed closed.

'… th-th-th-that!' Walter finished.

'You startled me,' said Alison.

'I'm c-c-c-c-clumsy.'

'It was an accident, I'm sure.'

There followed a long awkward pause with neither knowing what else to say. Finally, Allison broke the deadlock: 'Quite a game.'

Walter, startled at the conversation resuming, blurted: 'The All Blacks dominated the l-l-lineouts. T-t-t-twenty-five to th-thirteen. You c-c-can't have s-s-s-s-s-stats against you like th-th-that and hope to win.' Immediately a voice in his brain screamed, For God's sake, dickhead! Talk about something else! *Anything* else!!!

A complete blank – never had his mind been an emptier expanse.

To his amazement, the woman replied, 'Absolutely! Chris Jack was so right to be named Man of the Match. He and Williams were unstoppable. They picked off ten Lions throw-ins!'

Walter was stunned. He nodded, his mouth slightly agape.

This guy seems to know his rugby, thought Alison. She decided to press on. 'Mind you, the ABs have more than struggled with their own lineouts in recent years. So much so, in fact, that for a while there, when it wasn't their throw-in, they even stopped bothering to compete in the air. That was just stupid, staying on the ground! What a difference when they go for it and get it right. O'Connell and Kay didn't know what hit them!'

Walter stood and stared at her. Alison found it unnerving. Oh God, she thought, just shut up, Ali!

Silence prevailed again, which as time went by Alison found even more alarming. She foisted another fillip: 'Up front, the Lions had no real answers. The All Blacks attacked their feeds constantly and were pretty much unstoppable when it was their own put in.'

As an afterthought she added, 'And the Kiwis' ball-in-hand control was superb. You'd never have thought it was cold and raining throughout … the entire … match …' Her voice petered out as she heard herself and realised how long she'd droned on. She felt slightly sick.

Walter stood rooted to the ground, thunderstruck. The awkward stillness seemed to stretch on forever. Finally, from somewhere in his head, he at last heard something useful: *She knows rugby. She really knows the game! Just talk rugby with her!*

'Going with W-W-W-Wilkinson was always going to be a risk,' he said. 'His l-l-l-line-kicking didn't have distance. He l-l-l-lacked any power on runs up the m-m-middle. In f-f-f-fact, he added no r-r-r-r-r-r-r-rhythm to the backline at all!'

'Yeah,' replied Alison, without thinking, 'I reckon Sir Clive showed admirable faith in his World Cup match-winner, but it was always going to be a gamble. And now everyone knows it was misplaced.' She smiled. 'Can they take back knighthoods for that?'

Walter grinned.

And with that the two aficionados relaxed, and allowed their knowledge and enthusiasm full flight. They canvassed selection possibilities, probed the potential of different combinations, analysed the impact of injuries, and compared captaincies. Together, they made one almighty almanac. An hour flew by. Tables had been cleared and wiped, televisions switched off, glasses washed, extra staff sent on their way.

Alison looked about her and said, 'Well, thanks. It's been fun. But I've really got to go. I usually work Saturday mornings but I managed to get someone to change their afternoon shift with me.'

Walter nodded. He knew she'd have to leave sometime. He didn't know what to say.

'I won't be able to get a swap for the next two Tests, so I'll have to rely on my video at home.' Alison looked at Walter. She added with a forced smile: 'The Walkabout will just have to do without me.'

Walter was already feeling the pain of her departure. He really didn't know a thing about women, just that he was useless with them. But she was great, fantastic! She was smart, and funny, and sexy. And she didn't even seem to mind his stammer. She was too good to be true, and she was going now, and he felt helpless to do anything about it.

'So, maybe I'll see you around sometime,' said Alison. It was a closing. A closing, but an open-ended one – a test. If he's going to show me that he can see past my face, she thought, it's got to be now. Behind her back she crossed her fingers, on both hands.

Walter wanted to ask to see her again, with every fibre of his being. But what if he asked and she refused? What then? Oh God, how he'd feel! He could imagine her letting him down gently – she didn't seem a mean person. That's probably what all that swapping shifts story was about, he thought.

Alison felt her heart constricting. Over the years she'd steeled herself so well against pain and rejection. Why, oh, why had she let hope slip in? She felt the darkness rising up inside her like some denizen of the deep. It surged and billowed. It swam before her eyes, roiling and cresting. And then, with complete indifference, it swamped the brave, tiny, bobbing boat of desire. She blinked blindly.

Walter didn't see her struggle. He was staring morosely at his feet.

While she still had any voice left, Alison whispered, 'Goodbye, then.' Turning, she hurried from the pub.

Walter felt ashamed, disgusted with himself. Every taunt he'd suffered, every damning jeer, he now knew was utterly deserved. He *was* a loser, with a capital L!

A shhhhhhhhhhh of static caught Walter's attention, and he looked up to see the dark television screen directly in front of him flicker into life. Gauzy grey gave way to a close-up on the face of the New Zealand captain, Tana Umaga. His telltale dreads were tied back from his mocha-coloured face. He looked down at Walter and his Chinese-Polynesian eyes smiled.

'Hey, Walter, what are you doing? What are you thinking of, mate?'

Walter said nothing.

'You know, you didn't even ask her her name.'

Walter shifted uncomfortably.

The All Black continued: 'You can do this, Walter – look, you've got to. She *liked* you.'

Walter shook his head.

'She did, man! She liked you a lot!'

Umaga's stare went steely. 'Look, there comes a time in everyone's life when they've just got to step up to the mark.'

His eyes narrowed. 'Or live forever knowing the worst possible thing. Know what the worst possible thing is, Walter?'

Walter again shook his head.

'That they'll never ever know. Never know how things might have turned out.' He paused to let it sink in.

'You go for it, mate! Give it heaps! Because the alternative sucks: you'll never forgive yourself.'

Walter looked back down at his feet. He knew Tana was right. He knew this was his own personal half-time team talk. He had to pick up his game. He'd seen so many matches over the years won when they should have been lost. So much about winning was in the head of the players. Victory came to those who made it happen, those who wanted it badly enough.

Walter's back stiffened. He could do this!

He looked up again at the screen, but it was blank and mute like all the others. He turned on his heels and ran out the entrance into the middle of the road. He looked to his right. In the distance, beyond Waterloo Bridge and around a bend in the Thames, he could make out Big Ben and the Houses of Parliament. His eyes swept the footpaths. Nothing. He swung his head to the left, towards Blackfriars

Bridge. No sign of her at all. What if she'd gone into the tube? He'd never catch her then! He scanned the scene again, then a third time, with an ever-impending sense of doom.

He knew it – he'd left it too late! Failed, just like always! Lost, even with an All Black on his side! A taxi horn blared as the vehicle swerved to miss him. Walter yelled at its passing black shape: 'Fu-fu-fu-fu-fu-fu-fu-fu-fu-fu …' He couldn't even swear right! He was apoplectic with self-loathing.

Turning, he ran back into the pub, banging blindly into chairs and tables as he careened through the room. Facing the bank of lifeless televisions, Walter's face distorted in a rictus of rage. His hands tightened into fists that cuffed his head and tore at his hair. He screamed at the screens: 'D-d-d-d-dirty fu-fu-fu-fu-fuckin' l-l-l-l-liar! D-d-d-dirty fu-fu-fuckin' sh-sh-sh-sh-shitty l-l-l-l-l-l-liar!!!' Tears sprang forth. He sobbed, his body shuddering.

The few remaining pub workers watched the madness from afar, staying well back. Minutes passed in which Walter was utterly engulfed.

At last, his delirium spent, his weakened arms stilled to the occasional half-hearted lift, Walter sighed. It sounded grim and broken. The groan of complete dejection.

From behind, the touch of a hand on his shoulder. Walter jumped and swung around in alarm. His reddened eyes stared straight into Alison's worried face. She quickly, bravely put on a tentative smile.

'Guess what?' she said. 'We never even asked each other's names!'

THE CATHEDRAL

DEMONS DO DWELL in the house of God; they just hide where no one thinks to look – patiently biding their time, eternally waiting to spring.

Martin Chambers, his wife Nancy, and their two children, Zara, thirteen, and Bradley, nine, all look heavenwards as they make their way beyond the ticketing desk. Along the mighty length of the nave, under the massive dome, through the glittering quire, finishing in the distance above the high altar, it's all one huge, seemingly endless vista of geometric curvature.

'Wren had a thing about circles, didn't he?' says Zara, the straight-shooter of the family.

'Princess Diana got married here,' says Nancy brightly.

'For all the good it did her,' mumbles Zara.

'You know,' says Martin, 'there's been a church on this site since 604 AD. It was founded by St Mellitus, a follower of St Augustine, who had been sent to convert the Anglo-Saxons. Kind of puts our own church back home into perspective.'

'How old is our church, Dad?' asks Bradley.

Martin laughs and says, 'Oh, it goes way back – to let's see … um, 1978.'

'Its teachings, of course, go back to Jesus,' adds Nancy.

St Paul's isn't quite what they were expecting. In their three-month sojourn abroad from home in Sarasota, Florida, they have traveled through France, Spain, Italy, Greece, and now England. In every country they've made a point of visiting the great churches and cathedrals, with a view to presenting a vivid and uplifting report, upon their return, to the congregation of the Redemption Church of Christ Our Blessed Savior. Their idea has the enthusiastic support of their friend and pastor, Frank Mitchell. Martin takes photos of all the exteriors and, when allowed, the many and varied interiors, for the eventual slide presentation. Nancy, meanwhile, has been creating a series of poems written on-site whenever she feels inspired in the holy moment, which to Martin seems somehow far away here in this London landmark

'More like a museum than a church,' says Zara, echoing his thoughts. 'There's like a zillion statues of dead guys!'

'Cool,' says Bradley.

'Yes, but they're very famous dead guys,' says Martin, as they stand gazing up at Wellington's monument: an imposing study in black and white marble and bronze, with columns and arches and portals soaring powerfully upwards, and at the very top, astride it all, the horse-mounted Duke himself. 'They are remembered and celebrated in the many memorials around the cathedral. Poets, artists, war heroes, we're really in quite illustrious company!'

'Even Florence Nightingale,' says Nancy.

'And they're all buried right down below us,' says Martin, adding in a sinister voice, 'in the Cryyyyyypt.'

'Cool,' says Bradley.

Nevertheless, Martin knows what Zara means. He feels strangely unmoved. The Holy Spirit seems further away here than in any other church they've been to on their trip. Everything is so tidy and orderly, so calm and contained. Austere instead of awesome. There seems none of the grandiose exuberance evident throughout Italy; or the unexpurgated passion of the Spanish; or the earthy sacredness of Greece; or the stylish religious conviction of the French. No, this is all so … so … so British!

Nancy has once again found herself overcome with artistic reverie and is sitting down, pad in hand, scribbling feverishly. Martin's never had the heart to tell his wife what he really thinks of her writing. Faced with such unremitting amateurishness, the clumsiest of metaphors and most simplistic rhyming meters, he quells his gut reaction and remains loyally encouraging. He can't even begin to imagine what she's coming up with in this place.

Zara has shrugged them all off and is wandering the south transept, headphones on and eyes glued to her mobile phone; while Bradley meanders a disjointed course, stepping only on the black flags of the enormous expanse of checkerboard flooring.

Martin seizes the rare opportunity to move off and explore by himself. In the south quire aisle he finds the marble effigy of John Donne. He likes the idea that Donne had the foresight to wrap himself in a shroud and pose for its creation before he died.

On the other hand, he finds the recent Christ paintings

by Sergei Chepik in the nave, including the cathedral's first-ever depiction of the crucifixion, ugly and grotesque – all spiky angles, the figures sharply stretched and distorted.

As a US citizen he is impressed with the American Memorial Chapel in the apse. The Roll of Honour, a book containing twenty-three thousand names of Americans based in Britain during World War 2 who died on its behalf, is a simple, powerful remembrance.

Wandering around to the north transept Martin is delighted to discover William Holman Hunt's 'The Light of the World'. This Pre-Raphaelite vision of Christ standing in a doorway in an enchanted forest setting holding an exquisite Art Nouveau lantern simply shimmers. The pale halo shines forth against a deepening turquoise sky, while the mother-of-pearl gown, draped in a gold and red jewel-encrusted cape, gleams with His Holy presence. So far, the painting is the only thing Martin has seen in the entire cathedral that captures something of the frail beauty of his own personal spirituality.

While making his way along the north transept Martin encounters the carved memorial to Frederic Lord Leighton. The plaque reads: "… Painter, Sculptor, Seventh President of the Royal Academy of Arts … erected by his many friends and admirers. Born 3 Dec 1830, died 25 Jan 1896". In life-sized blackened bronze, the artist lies in his cape, forever asleep upon a swirl of green marble under the light filtering down from a vast multi-paned window above. He is at peace, but at his head and feet sit two carved bronze muses, styled totally in the manner of the 1920s, who seem very much alive. They each rest an arm on the plinth, perched and poised, forever vigilant to again inspire Leighton should he happen to arise refreshed from his slumbers and burst forth with yet another creative idea. The paintress holds a charged paintbrush, but it's the sculptress to whom Martin is irresistibly drawn. Not the woman herself, who grasps a carving tool in one hand, but what she holds in the other: a small carved male nude.

The figure is not ten inches high, but is so languorously posed in a standing stretch, as if just risen from bed, that Martin is riveted. The muscular right hip rises slightly, allowing the strong back to extend from taut buttock to square shoulder, arching in a firm yet easy sway. The left arm is coiled behind the man's gently modelled head, the right one tucks in under the tilted chin. The spread legs are relaxed but strong, simmering with a latent energy as if capable of bursting at a moment's notice into an effortless, endless run. Everything suggests indolent fluidity, but with a power and force behind it. To Martin, the allure of this gentle yet masculine vision is somehow beyond anything he has ever seen or imagined.

Bizarrely, he feels tears well in his eyes. Was there ever a form that so utterly captured the purity of true male loveliness? He can think of none, but then he can hardly think at all. He feels dizzy and short of breath. He blinks and his eyes spill over so that he peers into a veiled, watery world in which the figure seems to shift and shimmer and become invitingly alive. Joy, boundless and bursting with possibility, surrounds him, hugs him, as if it were the tiny bronze itself, grown life-size and wrapping its sweet strong arms about him. Martin hears a sob and a gasp and realises both have escaped from him.

'You know 'im then?'

'You like Lord Leighton?'

Martin's reverie is shattered. Gathering his wits he quickly wipes his eyes and turns to see a smiling buck-toothed man of about sixty gazing at him intently. He is a complete study in beige, from pants to cardigan to skin tone. His balding head is poorly disguised with a silvery comb-over. Neat and tidy, he looks like his mother has dressed him.

'Because you seem to be spendin'…'

'… a lot of time around 'is memorial.'

Martin is confused. Things are awry. Something is not quite right, but in the moment he can't put a finger on it. He stammers his reply: 'No. Ah, yes. Er, I mean … no, I don't really know him. And yes, I-I do like the memorial.'

'Sorry. Not pryin' or anythin' …'

'… just couldn't 'elp noticin'.'

'We like 'im too …'

'… 'is work and all.'

It dawns on Martin that he is turning his head from side to side, as each sentence ends and the next one begins.

'You been to Leighton 'ouse?'

'Over by 'olland Park?'

'Open to the public, it is …'

'… and well worth a visit!'

Why, Martin wonders, is he constantly looking from left to right, when the same man with the exact same voice speaks to him every time?

'We think 'e's the absolute stand-out …'

'… of all the Victorians. A giant!'

The man looks at the memorial for a moment, then back at Martin.

'Come to St Paul's often? We 'aven't been 'ere …'

'… for years. They've really cleaned it up.'

'It's lovely now!'

'Beautiful!'

At last the penny drops. Of course! Twins – he is talking to identical twins! They are dressed exactly the same. Martin feels the world turn right-side-up again.

'No, this is my first time here. We're visiting from America. Me, my wife and two children.'

'Oh, that's nice! We went to America ten years ago …'

'… to New York and New Orleans. Went on a steamboat …'

'… up the Mississippi. Loved it.'

'Loved it!'

As his head turns from one to the other, Martin warms to them, to their double act. 'I'm from Florida,' he says. 'No shortage of you Brits over there.'

'Got the right climate, you 'ave. We been talkin' …'

'… about goin' to Orlando for years.'

'Theme Park centre of the universe,' says Martin, and the twins nod their heads in unison.

'Probably best for little 'uns, though. But then …'

'… we never grown up ourselves!' They both laugh and Martin smiles.

'Do visit Leighton 'ouse though.'

'Interestin' … You'd enjoy it.'

'That small figure you been lookin' at …'

'… it's a copy of one of Leighton's most famous sculptures.'

'Got a name, it does. What's it called again?'

'Can't think right now. Name escapes me'.

'Never mind, it'll come. But Lord Leighton, 'e done the original.'

'In the Tate.'

'Bigger, of course …'

'… life-size.'

'*The Sluggard!*'

'That's it! Leighton called it *The Sluggard*.'

Martin coughs. 'I was admiring it.'

'Don' blame you one bit, mate …'

'… not a bit. It's a beautiful thing. Well, must dash.'

'Lovely meetin' you. 'ope you enjoy …'

'… the rest of your visit.'

'Cheerio,' they chirp in unison as they head off across the nave.

'Yeah, okay,' says Martin waving. 'So long.' And as an afterthought: 'Hope you make it to Florida.'

He turns back to the memorial, his eyes hungry to again devour the beautiful figure. He feels his heartbeat quicken and mouth go dry. He licks at his lips – and startles as Bradley pipes up from behind: 'Hey, Dad, they got stairs you can climb up that take you all the way to the top to a lookout! Can we go up?'

'Oh! Ah … sure thing, kiddo,' says Martin, feeling both

regret and relief at the intrusion. 'But let's find your mother and sister first, eh?'

The winding wooden stairs start out surprisingly wide, almost gracious in their expanse. Yet they are strangely shallow so that hidden muscles deep in the hip, the kind that never normally come into play, soon begin to ache dully. Bradley races ahead, Zara not far behind, but Nancy and Martin make heavier going of it. The stairs seem to stretch on forever. Eventually, two hundred and fifty-nine steps later, they reach the entrance to the Whispering Gallery.

'It's called that,' says Martin between breaths, '… because a whisper on one side … can be heard thirty-two metres away … on the other.'

Nancy, panting, nods and manages to say, 'Like the good Lord Himself.'

The children have already passed it by and continued their ascent, so Martin and Nancy decide to leave visiting it until the trip back down, and instead press on to the first-level lookout, the Stone Gallery. One hundred and nineteen considerably steeper, tightly winding steps later, at the very base of the massive dome, they stagger outside to a broad promenade. It is colonnaded around the periphery, through which can be glimpsed expansive views over the city. They stop and rest, pointing out various London landmarks while waiting for Bradley's and Zara's return from the top lookout, the Golden Gallery, another gruelling one hundred and fifty-two steps up.

When Bradley eventually bursts upon them he is full of

the triumph of his climb. 'It was really neat,' he exclaims. 'You sort of climb right over the top of the dome!'

Even the usually underwhelmed Zara seems enthusiastic. 'It went on, like, forever! And it was kinda creepy – I kept expecting to see Dracula or something.'

'Goodness!' exclaims Nancy. 'Never, in the house of the Lord!'

'Well,' says Martin, 'we two oldies have done our dash in the climbing stakes. Shall we go down and check out the Whispering Gallery?'

'Cool,' says Bradley.

As they all enter, their eyes automatically go up to the giant painted dome ceiling. Now, so much closer, it seems to writhe with decoration: classical figures, settings, architecture – a trompe-l'oeil world captured in sombre sepia and muted mushroom like some vast visual equivalent of a swirling whisper. A circular black rail skirts the bottom inside edge of the dome, preventing visitors navigating around the three-hundred-and-sixty-degree walkway from tumbling headlong into the enormity of the cathedral's gaping centre. Subdued hidden lighting from beneath the railing seems to add to the stillness, picking out the shadowy faces of those sitting against the side of the Dome on the continuous bench seating, or standing to peer the thirty metres down to the church floor below.

Martin immediately feels a sense of disquiet, the strange otherworldliness of the space. Sounds sluice and slide sideways around the circumference of the dome. Snatches of conversations, barely there, drift across the expanse into his awareness. He has an overriding need to be alone and sets off by himself. Nancy, meanwhile, has again delved into her handbag for pen and paper and sits writing determinedly.

Midway around, Martin sees appearing before him Leighton's marvellous sculpted man, now grown to superhuman size and floating in the air under the dome like an apparition, an angel. It could almost be a huge ascended Christ. Its arms stretch out, reaching towards him. Martin begins to stagger, his eyes filling with the unshed tears of so many unvoiced feelings. With a shudder he recognises what it is he is seeing, so rich and ripe in its utter rightness: Love. Man love. True love. Pure and unabashed, held not in check by sin or shame or disapproval, but vividly alive for all to see and marvel at. Martin holds his yearning arms up towards it. Nothing else in his life has ever felt so right, so perfect.

'Dad?' says Zara, approaching. 'What's wrong, Dad?'

Martin stumbles and clumsily feels behind himself for a seat. 'I just … just need to sit down for awhile,' he says.

'Are you … are you crying, Dad?'

'Leave me, Zara. Just go.' His daughter hesitates. 'Now, Zara. Now!'

Stung by her father's out-of-character sharpness, Zara backs off, slowly making her way around to her mother who still sits lost in her writing on the other side of the space, Bradley exploring nearby. Martin cups his hands over his face and weeps. He feels lost, bereft, trapped. He looks up and sees his beloved giant apparition hovering. They gaze upon each other with the sweet, tender pain of mutual longing.

He sucks in a shaky breath and whispers: 'I love you. I love you. I really do love you!'

He shakes his head, wrapping it, enclosing it in his arms. In misery he groans: 'I admit it. I love men. Beautiful, beautiful men. My life's a sham and there's nothing I can do about it.'

Out of the corner of his eye Martin notices Nancy in the distance, her head slowly rising from her notebook. He sees a strange look come over her face. What? Has Zara told his wife about his crying? Why is she staring at him? He sees Nancy's lips move and his hushed name spirals around the dome: 'M-Martin?' He hears her muffled, strained incredulity: 'My God, Martin – what did you just say?'

He looks into her eyes for what seems to be minutes, wincing as a blade twists and turns so deep in his stomach that he fears he will be sick. He glances up to the dome, catching a final glimpse of the evaporating vision: sorrow etched across its beautiful, fading face. Swallowing hard and burying forever the bittersweet tangle of terrifying urges, he faces his family and whispers louder: 'So, can you guys hear me over there? Earth to Nancy? Earth to Zara? Bradley?' He straightens his shoulders, drags composure back into his being. 'I sure hope you can hear me!' He manages a smile. 'Coz I'm absolutely starving! I gotta get outa here now and get some food into me – fast! Fast food! American food! Anyone care to join me at McDonalds?'

He watches Nancy's mouth struggle. Bradley grins at him. Zara watches cautiously.

'Oh – and hey, you guys, I was just saying before: I love you, I really do love you!'

He sees Nancy's eyes trained on him. For the briefest of moments they flash, cold and hard as the endless polished marble that so abounds in this house of worship. Then her lips move. Softly, faintly, her words snake across the void: 'We love you too', they hiss. 'God bless you, Martin.'

THE ESTATE

THE FOOTPATHS AND gutters are strewn with empty crisps packets, plastic shopping bags, sheets of newspaper and junk mail, fag ends, a child's cardigan, a single running shoe, crushed Carling cans, and a scattered pack of flaccid johnnies, empty as a quick fuck.

Mary Stensness guides her trailing blue zip-around case, knuckles tightly gripping the extended handle, as she weaves her way around the careless clutter of urban jetsam and flotsam, carefully avoiding the slightest contact. Such filth, she thinks. Still, it's but a short walk from the underground through these unkempt streets of the estate. And although she finds such degradation and disregard just one more example of the ever-lowering tone of the species, Mary purses her lips and pushes on, for she knows she is made of sterner stuff.

Before pressing the doorbell, Mary checks the house number one final time from the text the agency has sent her. She can just detect the bell's muffled ring from somewhere inside. She waits. Three hours earlier she was in Nottingham, finishing a four-week stint with an elderly couple challenged in their final years by the double-surname whammy of Parkinson's and Alzheimer's. With her Notts changeover completed, Mary caught the 11a.m. train to St Pancras, then hopped the tube to arrive three blocks away from where she now stands, still waiting at the door.

It takes a full two minutes before a banging and clattering on the other side announces the arrival of someone. She hears the latch thumped and flicked at a few times before it springs open. Mary looks straight ahead, expecting the eyes of the other caregiver to welcome her – then tilts her glance downwards as she notices a head at the same height as her ample hips, struggling to peer around the partially opened door. There is more clatter as the wheelchair backs away down the passage to allow the door to open fully. Mary adjusts her surprise and puts on an earnest smile. 'Hello. I was expecting your caregiver to answer,' she says. 'You must be Robert.'

Rob Fraser, thirty-five, looks up at his temporary caregiver for the next two weeks, sent by the agency to replace Terry, his usual one, who is off to the Lake District for a much-needed break: the 24/7 nature of the work can certainly take its toll. Rob figures she must be sixty if she is a day, dressed smartly in her green drill skirt and matching jacket, and white, frilly-collared blouse, buttoned up and anchored firmly at the top under a cascading set of chins. Her eyes are small and bright, almost steely, as is her hair, back-combed and coiffed with lashings of hairspray.

'I'm Mary,' she declares with gusto, as if all the mysteries of the world are at last revealed. 'Mary Stensness.' She reaches in and takes a twisted hand from Rob's lap and pumps it vigorously. Startled, his head momentarily jerks sideways, then comes back under control, as he shuffles his feet to move his wheelchair backwards until she lets go of his hand.

He manages a wary smile and says, 'Ehh-oh. Ow wuh eor rip?'

'Oh dear, oh dear,' tisks Mary. 'I didn't catch a word of that! Still, I'll get an ear for it soon enough.' She looks around the hallway then directs her tiny eyes back at Rob. 'Has your caregiver left already? We're supposed to have an hour's changeover.'

Rob nods in agreement to both points. He takes a breath and offers up an explanation: 'Erry ag an op-er's appoimen.' Mary blinks and looks at him. Rob tries again, 'E ag oo go an ee er op-er.' Mary shakes her head. Rob's head bends and his neck twists and his arms twitch with effort: 'Op-er! E ag oo go an ee er op-er!'

'Do you have a stroke chart?' asks Mary.

Rob sighs and kicks his feet out and the wheelchair careens backwards around a corner into the sitting room. Rob then leans forwards and walks his chair, after a fashion, towards the small dining table. He swings his arm in the direction of a glass vase and Mary sees, leaning up against it, the stiff folded card covered in large capital letters. She lays the card flat on the table and holds it securely so Rob can thump his wildly extended forefinger onto the letters: D – O – C – T – O – R.

'Ahhh,' says Mary, smiling in triumph, 'he had to go and see the doctor! He had an appointment, did he?' Rob smiles in relief, but Mary purses her mouth. Rob notices how much it resembles a tight little arsehole. 'Well, it's certainly not good to not have a proper changeover! There's a lot I need to know about the set-up here!'

'We aah a wi-ee-oh oo an wah.'

'Pardon?'

'A wi-ee-o!' Rob repeats. 'We aah a wi-ee-oh!'

'Spell please, Robert.'

Rob pounds out: V – I – D – E – O. 'Wi-ee-o!' he says.

'Oh. You have a video I can watch! You've made a video for the changeover. How enterprising, Robert!'

'Ob,' says Rob. 'I ame i Ob.' He reaches to the chart and spells out: R – O – B. 'At's I ame. Eryone alls ee Ob.'

Mary smiles benevolently. 'So it's Rob. You like to be called Rob. Well, that's just fine. Now, let's watch this video, shall we, Rob? Then you can show me to my room. I'll need to change my clothes. There's no doubt much for me to be getting on with.'

Rob smiles back – he looks tired.

The days are highly structured. Routines and timings are in place that serve Rob well. Much of the time he seems content to merely wheel himself about from room to room in the house or out into the back garden. He sings strange little songs to himself, halflings actually, for they are largely tuneless and the words indecipherable. Mary busies herself in and around Rob's considerable needs: his personal grooming, preparing their three meals a day and washing up afterwards, keeping the house clean, doing the laundry, making the beds, venturing to the nearest shops for any top-up shopping, and squeezing in her scheduled daily breaks. She is unhappy that the usual agency allotment of a two-hour spell to herself each day is, by necessity, here split into two one-hour periods, one in the morning and one in the afternoon.

This is due to Rob's need for assistance on and off the toilet. He drinks so much tea throughout the day from his straw and mug placed on a mat at the near edge of the dining table that he seldom gets past an hour without calling out, 'Ary! Oiyet!' And Mary hurries to help guide his wheelchair into the bathroom, to the front of the toilet where she undoes his pants, bends down so he can drape his waving arms around her neck and then supports him to stand up from his wheelchair. He totters on skewed feet until he grasps hold of the specially installed side support rail, while Mary pulls down his pants and underpants, lifts his shirt tail, and steers his bum onto the toilet seat as he perilously throws himself down upon it from standing. She then exits, while he opens his legs and jolts his body about until his penis falls between them, pointing safely into the bowl. Sometime later a cry of 'Ary' brings her back to assist him to his feet again, so she can pull up his underpants and pants, tuck in his shirt, do up his pants and shuffle him around till he can sit back down in his wheelchair. Invariably, within minutes, comes the request: 'Up uh ee?' and she heads into the kitchen to make him yet another cup of tea, thereby assuring the cycle never ends.

Toileting can occur up to a dozen times a day, and Mary finds as the day progresses that it steadily drains her energy. She is used to having transfer aids such as turning plates or hoists to assist with lifting – Rob is a big man and she is dismayed at the lack of them here. He has explained that they are on back-order following a recent, long-overdue visit by the assessors at social services. She is unhappy about it, but reminds herself that it's only for two weeks.

One bonus is that Rob's toilet is equipped with a special bidet system that he operates by leaning his back against a lever on the cistern. This removes the necessity for Mary to wipe his bottom or deal with bowel motions. Not that Mary would flinch at the prospect – she's an experienced caregiver. And besides, she's always prided herself on the empathy she feels for the brave struggles of her clients. After all, it's there but for the grace of God that she herself might be.

Still, by the end of the second day she realises this placement is taxing beyond anything she has previously dealt with. Mary climbs into her bed at 11:30p.m., exhausted. She is asleep within minutes, but not before she reminds herself that she's made of sterner stuff.

Deep within the warm amniotic fluids is life absolute: seminal and perfect. It is from here that the small shell-like ears form, the dark stain of eyes, the snub of nose and tiny Mona Lisa mouth. And the ever-growing shape-shifting skin, permanently wet and more akin in this watery world to that of a dolphin. Nothing to hear save the ever-present beat of the mother drum, the occasional rush of liquids, the murmur of muffled voices. Nothing to see in this endlessly darkened realm. Nothing to smell or taste. Nothing to feel but the soft press against yielding organs and the shielding underside of overarching ribs. Senses primed and gradually readied in this safest of all places. Life will never again offer such languid shelter. No knowing, no understanding – no need for either. Abyss. Bliss.

Hence no recognition of the slowly developing tangle. No awareness of the gentle, frightful sailor's knot. No alarm as the cord pulls ever tighter around the neck – constantly, inexorably, day by day. Until at last, birth, when waves burst and worlds tumble in a pushing, pulling, squeezing frenzy. And in the final maelstrom – those fateful, perilous minutes – the blackout. The temporary blasphemy of blood blocked from the brain.

"I'm sorry to have to tell you this, Mrs Fraser, Mr Fraser, but it appears that your son …" Mary wakes with a jolt. She sees the glow of 3:34 a.m. on her travel alarm. Her pillow is damp, she realises she has been crying in her sleep. Oh, she sobs, you poor, poor thing. You poor wee darling.

Every other day is bathing day, which means every other day is more gruelling than the one preceding or following it. The hydraulic tilting bath eases things considerably, but nevertheless the sessions are long, hot and wearying. First, there's the toilet, of course. While the bath fills, the latex gloves are pulled on. Hearing aids are switched off and removed. Then, the untying and removal of shoes and socks. The peeling off of the t-shirt, like skinning a possum except that with the arms waving about so much it's as if the animal is still alive, clinging obstinately to life. This is followed by the dreaded lifting procedure, so that pants and underpants can be dropped around the feet. Then back down into the chair, which then gets wheeled across to the bath.

With its sidewall lifted, Rob is again stood up and shimmied around to be set down on the bath's raised seat. Here pants and underpants are pulled off before the legs are lifted over the edge and into the water. The bath side is dropped back down and locked watertight. The handle is swung out and pumped so that bit by bit the bath tilts backwards, lowering Rob until his sitting position becomes largely horizontal. As he sinks, the warm water from the filled deep area around his feet rushes in, flows over and around his body. His tense frame visibly eases – its involuntary jerks and shudders, for a blessed spell, are stilled. Rob sighs and shuts his eyes in delight. Mary sighs and shuts hers in grim determination.

The next thirty minutes will see Mary hunched over, soap and flannel in hand, meticulously washing every nook and cranny of Rob's body. She will wash and rinse his hair, his face, his waxy ears. She will wash his armpits, his chest, his back. She will wash his hands, carefully wiping around stiff, extended fingers, so flagrantly arched back upon themselves they'd be the envy of any traditional Thai dancer. She will lift and wash each leg. Each foot. She will slide her arm fully underwater to clean his bottom. She will, oh so gently, wash his testicles, as they slide freely about in their softened sac. And his limp floating penis.

By the time the bath has been tilted upright and drained, and Rob towel-dried as best as possible in situ, then stood up and returned to his chair, taken into his bedroom, stood up and laid onto his bed on a towel, dried fully and talc applied, clean socks pulled on, clean underpants pulled on, pants pulled on, stood up again and seated back in the wheelchair, deodorant rolled on, clean shirt pulled over head, wandering, simian arms negotiated into sleeves, hair blow-dried and combed, ears dried and hearing aids put back in and switched on … by the time Mary reaches this point, her back is aching to near seizure and she can think of only one thing: her blessed one hour of relief, when she will lay flat on her bed, infused with aspirin, waiting for the searing pain to ease. But before this, the relentlessly inevitable alert: 'Ary! Oiyet!'

In the evening Mary stands slumped at the kitchen bench. She has cooked their meals, kept hers warm in the oven while she fed Rob his, and then eaten her own. Now she tends to the washing up, staring out the kitchen window to the small back garden growing ever gloomier in the falling dusk. Bone weary, she measures the mounting wear and tear on her physical and emotional being. She knows the life force is beginning to drain from her, feels it dripping, slipping, fading away. Nodding off, her eyes close and her head dips briefly, only to start and rise, then dip again. Her dish-gloved hands feel so heavy. Slowly they slide to a sudsy standstill.

It is three years earlier, and Mary's husband of twenty-five years, Bill, a pharmaceutical sales rep, has just upped and left, abandoning her for a woman half his age. With the house in his name, he has promptly sold it, taken his part of the proceeds and absconded in less than two months. All he would say, when bewildered Mary asked, amid seemingly endless tears, over and over again, 'Why? Just tell me why?' were four chilling words: 'The love is gone.' She knows now it was his love for himself that had gone. Replaced by that clichéd crisis that befalls so many men who, in the plain face of their mortality, flee it. Pot bellies, balding heads and twilight-careers making them suckers for the one symbol they can trick themselves with, believing they are somehow stemming the tide: a younger woman's flesh.

Bill and his tiny-waisted Tina now live in an apartment in Benidorm in Costa Blanca. Simon and Timothy, Mary and Bill's two grown-up sons, both live abroad, one in France, the other in Stockholm. Initially, loyally, they were incensed on their mother's behalf, but over time they proved themselves far more willing than she to forgive their father his sudden change. Mary prides herself that she never succumbed to out-and-out rage. She's always known what she was made of. So she dried her tears and got on with it.

To support herself she needed to find work, not an easy thing for an ex-housewife in her late fifties. In The Lady magazine Mary found a raft of advertisements for live-in caregivers. The various agencies seemed to offer exactly what she needed: financial security, purpose, and a roof — albeit an ever-changing one — over her head. She applied to one of the biggest companies, completed their training and stepped bravely into her new life.

'Sterner stuff,' she mumbles from her sink-side slumber, 'sterner stuff.'

Caregiver changeovers occur midweek. Five days on, it is their first Sunday together. Mary sits feeding Rob his lunch: baked beans on toast, banana, Ribena. In spite of her tired and stiff frame and increasingly addled thinking, she suggests to him that he might enjoy a nice walk afterwards to the shops. The day is warm and not too sunny, it would do him good to get out. Rob agrees. Mary attaches the footrests, usually removed so that Rob can use his feet to move his wheelchair about, and puts a cardigan on him in case things go suddenly cool.

Pushing him up the road, she takes great care to ease any bumps and jolts. They spend an agreeable hour looking in a scruffy assortment of nearby £1, discount and clearance stores. Mary buys a peppermint chocolate bar and slips single squares into Rob's smiling mouth.

That evening, as Mary tucks Rob into his bed, tightly so that he can't fall out during sleep, she smiles at him and says loudly, since his hearing aids have been removed to the dresser for the night: 'It was a nice day, wasn't it.'

Rob replies, 'Uh huh.'

'We're doing alright, aren't we, Rob?'

He smiles and says, 'Ou are ery ice, Ary. I ike ou.'

Mary's heart fills with warmth. 'You sleep tight, and mind the bedbugs don't bite!' and she switches off the light. Neither of them recognise this moment as the zenith of their relationship, the crest of their companionship.

Monday morning and Mary is up and dressed when she is called, as usual, into Rob's bedroom between 7 and 7.30a.m. by the startling scream of the intercom alarm, placed on the wall within striking distance of his flailing left arm. She quickly swallows the last of her cup of tea and hurries to him.

Upon opening the curtains she discovers Rob holding up his hand to show her blood on it. There is also blood on his face, in his hair and on his pillow, and a light smear across the top edge of his sheet and duvet. 'Rob!' she exclaims. 'Oh my, what's happened?' Her fears are quickly allayed when she realises Rob has scratched his ear in the night. She examines his ear, then his stained fingers. 'You're okay,' she bellows. 'You've simply scratched yourself. My goodness, these nails are long! Today's bath day, so I'll give them a trim afterwards, eh? Now, let's get some tissues and clean you up a bit.'

At breakfast, Mary is feeding Rob his cornflakes when he tells her, 'Ary, I ike ou oo ane er eets.'

'What is that, Rob?'

'I ike ou oo ane er eets.'

'You'd like me to …?'

'Er eets,' Rob explains. 'Osh an ane er eets ease, Ary.'

'Er eets? Oh, the sheets! The sheets, Rob? Wash and change the sheets?'

'An er uvet uver,' Rob adds, noticing Mary's sudden sour grimace.

She cannot even countenance the thought of dealing with Rob's king-size bed today. She's zeroed out – running on empty. She knows there is no way she can manage more. 'I don't think I can today, Rob. Not on top of everything else on bath day. I'll change your pillowslips, of course, but how about I leave stripping and making up the rest of the bed until tomorrow?'

Rob's face clouds, and Mary has a sinking feeling. He shakes his head.

'But I'm exhausted!' Mary blurts out, before she has time to catch herself.

'Ut ou are y areiver, Ary,' says Rob.

Mary's eyes harden. For the briefest of moments she thinks of all her years of marriage, how she cared, day in, day out, for her husband's and sons' every endless need. How she was always there for them. How each, in their way, deserted her – put themselves, their lives, ahead of her own.

'Of course I am, Robert. I am your caregiver. That's what I do. I don't know what came over me. You shall have them.' The rest of the meal is conducted in stony silence, except for the unusually loud clacking of spoon on teeth as Mary feeds Rob the remainder of his cornflakes. And so it begins.

Tuesday

'Why Robert,' says Mary, when she sees his full, now cold cup of tea, 'you didn't touch your tea, that's not like you at all.'

'Oo ar away,' says Rob.

'What's that, Robert?'

'Oo ar away!'

'No good, Robert. We'd better use the chart.'

Rob sighs. He struggles to spell out: T – O – O F – A – R A – W – A – Y.

'Toofa raway? What language is that, Robert! You're not making any sense.'

Rob shakes his head in dismay and laboriously spells it out again.

Mary suddenly gushes, 'Oh, I see. How terribly remiss of me! I left your tea in the middle of the table before I went out for my break. I really am sorry, Robert.'

Wednesday (Day 1 of Week 2)
Bath day again. Mary swings Rob's legs around and into the water. A strange panicked gurgling escapes from his throat as he struggles to jerk his legs up out of the burning water. Mary can see, behind his large pupils, the frightened whites of his eyes, like those of a cornered animal, as he looks at her in alarm. 'Oh, I'm sorry, Robert. Is that a bit hot? I must be more careful!'

Thursday
Rob chokes on the mackerel Mary has prepared and is now feeding him at dinnertime, his eyes squeezed closed and neck muscles straining as he leans forward to hack and cough. 'Oh dear, Robert! Fish bones? I really thought I'd got them all,' says Mary, as she wipes off his trembling chin. She notices, as he continues to sputter, how surprisingly like a mackerel his own extended mouth appears.

Friday
'Ary! Oilet!' Robert calls from the bathroom, over and over again, each time louder and with greater urgency. 'Oilet!!!' By the time Mary gets to him, explaining as she enters the room just how hard it is to hear him from the kitchen when the washing machine is going, Rob sits in silence, head bowed and shoulders slumped. On seeing the dark wet patch across

his lap, Mary says, 'Oh, Robert, really! Mind you, if you didn't drink so much tea!'

Saturday

Mary enjoys a morning lie-in. She rises at a leisurely 9:45 and makes herself a nice cup of tea. After she has dressed she ventures into Rob's bedroom. 'Oh my, Robert, look at the time. See here, your intercom has somehow come unplugged at the wall – no wonder I overslept!'

Sunday

'Ary, I an ou oo eave,' says Rob. It is the middle of the afternoon. He is watching Mary, who sits humming, doing the crossword in the Sunday paper.

'What's that Robert?' she replies absent-mindedly.

'I an ou oo eave!' he says again.

'Leave? Why, I am leaving, Robert, in three days' time.'

'O!' Rob exclaims shaking his head determinedly. His legs and arms are jolting and swinging in agitation. 'Ou eave ow!'

'Why on earth should I leave now, Robert?' asks Mary, still looking at her crossword.

'O away!' Rob screams. 'O away!'

Mary looks up from the paper. 'On Wednesday I will leave.' A slow smile spreads across her face. 'Just three more days, Robert. After all, I can't just up and go. I am your caregiver.'

THE HOLIDAY

IN LATE SEPTEMBER the autumnal wind, the Meltima – that cyclonic Cycladic belter out of the northeast – sends tourists scurrying into sheltered spots on the still-sun-drenched beaches, and culls the usual free-flow of ferries to and from the island. The stout Cubist dwellings dotting the stony landscape, aglow with walls of bleached white, and doors and shutters of sensuous cyan, take it in their stride. They've weathered these annual extremes for centuries. They are like the people themselves: sturdy, practical, and resigned to a life of cycle upon cycle.

Mykonos: island of tiny chapels and towering cruise ships, wandering shepherds and bass-booming beaches. Island of opposites. In the Hora, the harbour town centre, the cunning locals of long ago joined all of their buildings together, interwove them in an endless array of alleyways and passages. Today, lined with trendy boutiques, restaurants, bars and galleries, the car-less walkways charm and beguile the hordes of visitors. A far cry from their original purpose: to blind and confuse preying pirates who would find themselves hopelessly lost in the identical-looking labyrinthine lanes.

Mykonos: crowded like crazy through the northern summer, but now, like an unruly child brought into line, becoming calmer, quieter, with each passing day.

She sits and watches the scudding clouds, the sudden blasts of wind that here, near the shore, sweep the sea's surface in rippling fans like giant invisible hands stroking turquoise velvet. In the distance the deeper navy-blue water dances, driven with the spray of millions of whitecaps.

She observes the few post-summer visitors dotting the beach: they turn their faces away and rub at their legs as they are peppered with sudden blasts of shore-shot sand. Hard to believe that only a fortnight before this place was teeming with masses of tanning bodies of every conceivable size and shape, from so many distant shores: rotund Germans, apologetic Poles, snobbish Italians, circumspect Japanese, chattering Greeks of course, and the inevitable groups of Americans with their loud questions and hardy hellos. Even with numbers now thinning, she still sees sitting among the straights a few gay couples, remarkably restrained here on San Stefano beach, unlike the outrageously uninhibited antics paraded night and day on the frenzied, beat-driven dance beaches on the southern side of the island: Paradise and Super Paradise, both more like hell in the high season.

Gentle San Stefano, with its small sweep of bay, just minutes from Hora by shuttle bus, has been her home away from home for the past twenty-three years. Her annual pilgrimage to its shores now a part of the very fabric of her life. She loves its lack of self-aggrandisement, its quieter, easier pace; its few older, non-brand-name hotels, and the huddle of small tavernas at the beach's far end. All watched over by an ever-growing sprinkling of sumptuous private homes dotting the dry, flinty hills above.

It is the afternoon before she is due to return to her quiet life in London, where she lives alone in a small downstairs flat near Battersea. Retired now, after years of what they once termed 'special teaching', she has spent the bulk of her working life calming down challenged and challenging children from their sudden feral outbursts of frustration. She has enthused over their smallest, most arcane of academic gains; their struggling smeared words and slurred conversations; their staccato grunts of concentration and sudden inexplicable fits of delirious laughter. It was a shock, at first, but she got over her original alarm and grew to love them, in her detached and undemonstrative way.

But that's all in the past. Now, with so much time on her hands, she fills her days with the lonely arts: exhibitions in the nearby Pump House Gallery in Battersea Park, afternoon pictures at the National Film Theatre, evening productions at the Old Vic and concerts at the Barbican. She would never call herself a cultural junkie, but if nothing else London teems with such diversions, and the many shows and performances serve their purpose well: they fill her days and nights. And once a year, every year, for six weeks at a time, she departs the city, flies direct to Athens, and makes the three-and-a-half-hour ferry sailing to Mykonos.

She leaves the beach early to go to her room and pack her case. She likes to have everything ready the night before departure so she can sleep assured. There is a ritual attached to all of this: first she must put her shoes in the bottom of the bag, followed by any dirty clothing she hasn't had time to wash in the bathroom sink, and her damp swimming costume wrapped in a plastic bag.

Then go in any breakables, padded over with a layer of soft tops and cardigans, followed by, to the left, underwear, bras and socks, and to the right, shorts and pants. Next, the books she's been reading: always biographies, of lives impossibly extravagant (Grace Kelly) or challenging (Helen Keller) or commanding (Joan d'Arc), topped off by her wash bag, with its coterie of travel medicaments and odd few gestures towards cosmetic artistry.

And finally, the small framed picture that she carries with her wherever she travels: a black-and-white photograph of herself aged ten years. How proudly she sits, her young chin held high and her clear eyes wide open. Her eyes engage the camera somewhat alarmingly, so unflinching are they in her bright, young countenance; her fresh-faced innocence and self-confidence.

As she sets the frame on top of the bag's neatly aligned contents, she pauses to draw a finger around the contours of her youthful face, outlining her past. 'Dear sweet thing,' she says in a filtered, far-off voice, before slowly, gently closing the case and zipping it tight.

She has made the Aphrodite Hotel her sole holiday bivouac all these years, so that now she is regarded virtually as one of the family. For indeed the Aphrodite is a family-run affair, overseen with unquestioned authority by the widow Abraxia. Resolutely, she sits planted in the small kitchen, dressed always in the black peasant robes of another era, a reminder of the Greece so rapidly disappearing from modern times. Abraxia could not possibly cope without her dear son, Demetri, a sublime and unruffled man of thirty-eight years. It is Demetri who, with the stealth of an Athenian cat, does the incessant running around, keeping the hotel humming: seeing to check-ins and check-outs, ensuring rooms are cleaned, bed-linen changed, bookings made, excursions planned, breakfasts served, small bar stocked, doors mended, shower leaks plugged; and always answering guests' endless questions with unrivalled politeness and an inscrutable smile.

The Aphrodite, having once been the only hotel in San Stefano, enjoys prime position in front of the sandy beach, separated from it only by the worn strip of road that welcomes the rattling, old shuttle bus every half-hour. Now, with the season almost closed, apart from the occasional buzz of a passing scooter or quad bike, things are largely quiet.

On this, her last night, she decides to head into Hora for a going-away meal. Getting off the bus she makes her way along the waterfront. A slow dusk is descending and the lights from the shops and cafés across the small inner harbour reflect over the water, dancing at the edges of bobbing fishing boats. She passes the tiny fishermen's church perched just metres from the shore and turns left to wander along one of the winding pathways leading uphill and over to the other side, to a cluster of buildings perched dramatically on the water's edge: Little Venice, named for the brightly painted homes of long-deceased sea merchants, the buildings' sheer sides dropping directly into the waves.

These days the old homes are filled with bars and restaurants and scuttling waiters who squeeze through crowds holding trays high above their heads. It is a place she'd never dream of going to in the high season, amid the din of hundreds of hungry mouths briefly escaped from the visiting harbour-anchored floating hotels, their decks aglow with strings of pretty lights. But with the coming of autumn the rabble has disappeared and Little Venice enjoys an unlikely few weeks of calm and composure before shutting down entirely for the winter months.

She orders a gin and tonic and the stuffed baby squid, and asks specially for the candle on her table to be lit. The sea slaps not two feet from her table, gradually merging with the deepening oily blackness of night. She has a second drink, and slips her cooling arms into the cardigan draped over her shoulders.

'Excuse me, I couldn't help noticing you seem to be alone.'

She looks up into the face of a smiling man in his mid-fifties, and then turns in her seat to check behind her, wondering who it is that he is addressing.

'I know that sounds like a pick-up line,' he laughs.

This is unprecedented. She says nothing, but pulls her cardigan tighter to her chest.

'I'm sorry — I have offended you. Please forgive me.' The man turns to move away.

To her surprise she finds her voice: 'No … no, you just startled me. I was miles away. Why do you want to know if I am alone?'

The man turns back. 'I don't know, really. I'm not in the habit of approaching strange women. Not that you are strange! What I mean is, women who I don't know. It's just that I was sitting over there and found I could not take my eyes off you.' He shakes his head. 'And that sounds like a pick-up line, too.'

She studies his face, tries to assess the honesty behind the words. His eyes are kindly. She decides to be candid: 'Well, I'm certainly not in the habit of being approached by strange men.' She smiles. 'Not that you're strange.'

'And yes, I am alone,' she adds.

His eyes crinkle. 'Then may I be a step bolder and ask that I might join you? Buy you another drink?'

She pauses, assessing this most unusual situation. Then she decides: 'Yes, you may join me. And no, I've had enough to drink, thank you.'

'A coffee perhaps?'

'No, thank you.'

He sits opposite her. 'You are English.'

'Yes, I'm from London. And you are … Greek?'

'Athens born and bred. Of course, like half of Greece I spend the summer months in the islands. You've been to Mykonos before?'

'Oh yes, many times. I know it well.'

'And where are you staying?'

'At San Stefano Beach.'

'Why that is where I have my holiday home, at the top of the cliffs – it's just along from the small chapel with the red door.'

'I know the one,' she says.

'And you always come by yourself to Mykonos?'

She touches her hair self-consciously and looks to the sea. 'Yes.'

'Why, an attractive woman like you, alone?'

She smiles. 'You sure you haven't done this sort of thing before?'

'Madam, until a year ago I was a happily married man. Then my wife died of a stroke. It was mercifully quick, bless her soul. But please do believe me when I say I have not thought of another woman for many, many years.'

'I'm sorry. I'm really very sorry for your loss.' She shakes her head. 'I guess I just can't understand why you're thinking now … of me.'

He smiles and shrugs apologetically: 'These things are sometimes the way of life, are they not?'

They look at each other, measuring things up. Finally, she again surprises herself by volunteering: 'Look, I'm a woman just this side of sixty. I've never married. I can't begin to remember how many years it's been since I last dated anyone. I live by myself. I'm used to a very tidy, very ordered existence. And I really don't want anything, or any *one*, to come along and mess things up.'

She pauses, then continues: 'Frankly, you're scaring me somewhat. And before you protest, let me say it is nothing you are doing. You seem to be a nice man, a charming man. But I'm thrown by this. And I just …' She sighs. 'I guess I just need you to know that.'

She is visibly shaking after her outburst. He says nothing

for a long time. Finally, he catches her eye and asks, 'What is your name?'

'Marjorie. My name is Marjorie. And yours?'

'Stavos.' Again, a long pause. Then he tilts his head to one side and says, 'Marjorie, may I ask you, please, one single question?' She nods. 'If you knew you were to die tomorrow, that everything would come to an end, then how would you choose to spend tonight?'

'That's a loaded question, if ever there was.'

'Are you able to, do you think, answer it?'

'I don't believe I can.'

'Well, perhaps you'll allow me to answer the same question?'

'Let me guess, in my arms?' She immediately regrets the cynicism of her retort and watches him, awaiting its impact.

She is surprised at the relief she feels seeing his smile. 'But of course. I would want to share my final hours in an embrace.'

'But you don't even know me. You know nothing about me.' Again she notices the unusual sharpness in her comeback. This is not a joust, she reminds herself.

'That is precisely what I would value about the time, however brief. The opportunity to get to know you. Intellectually, emotionally,' he smiles, and for the first time he looks almost bashful, 'physically.'

I'm past all this, she thinks. This is some Mills and Boon holiday nonsense. I need to go to bed. Alone! I need to get some sleep for tomorrow's journey. Yet she finds herself feeling tingly, nervously alive. For the third time she is surprised at the words that leave her lips: 'Yes, I can see that. That would be a lovely way to spend your last night on earth.'

They make their way to Taxi Square and leave Hora for San Stefano. It is late and all is dark and quiet when they arrive, pulling into his gated driveway. As the car departs, he says, 'It's cooler now – please allow me to give you my jacket', and without waiting for her response he places the coat over her shoulders. It is still warm from his body. From the collar she detects hints of a sweet and woody scent. 'Allow me, please, to show you my view.'

He leads her by the arm up to the house, around the paved, covered porchway, past hanging bougainvillea and the glowing blue oblong of a swimming pool, to where in the distance, like a small misshapen galaxy, shimmer the twinkling lights of Hora.

'Oh,' she breathes. 'It's very beautiful. Lovely.'

He gazes out to sea. 'Yes. In a world gone mad we need serenity and beauty, don't you think? Somewhere to be a step removed.'

'This is quite a step.'

He smiles. 'Maybe for us both. But yes, I am a lucky man, to have this house, with this view, on this island. And now, this moment.' He looks at her. 'How about that drink, now? White wine perhaps?'

Later in the bedroom, as she removes her clothes, she hears a voice inside her that keeps saying: this can't be happening to me, this is what happens to other people, not me. This is crazy. Surely this is all a dream. She slides between the sheets. The satin is cool against her skin. She turns on her side, tucking her arm under her head, and looks out the floor-to-ceiling windows at the dark vista and far-off glimmer. She is strangely calm, aware of how odd it is that she's not a bumbling mass of nerves. When you don't have much to start with, you don't have much to lose, she tells herself. This must be why I am so relaxed.

He enters from the bathroom, naked. Removed from his well-tailoured clothes he seems smaller now, with a childlike swell to his belly. She notices how the hairy patch on his chest is liberally sprinkled with grey. He sits on the bed next to her, kindly, she assumes, for what seems to be many minutes before finally touching her.

He begins by lightly massaging her shoulders. It feels good, soothing, so unexpectedly right. Her skin awakens under his touch, luxuriates in slowly coming alive. A lifetime, she thinks, I've spent a lifetime away from this, and she begins to weep silently. He seems to understand – he says nothing but carries on rubbing tenderly. When at last he senses the tears have stopped, he eases her flat onto her stomach and begins to stroke up and down the length of her spine. 'Mmmmm,' she groans, and he laughs softly. He gently kneads at the soft flesh spilling to either side of her shoulder blades and she feels the first faint warm stirrings deep within her womb. I can't believe this is happening to me!

A few more minutes pass before he softly presses his warm lips into the small of her back. The delicate, delightful flutterings slowly make their way up her spine. At last he leans over her and lightly places his hands on either side of her neck, ready to ease her over onto her back.

The hands are rough, cold and harsh, the nails thick and chipped. They scratch and grapple and grasp. The left hand clamps down on the back of her neck, pinning her so tightly to her bed that she can't even draw a breath to scream. The right hand, meantime, has forced its way down into her pajama bottoms and fumbles and scrapes between her legs. She fights. She squirms. She kicks. But she cannot breathe, the pillow jams into her open mouth. Her strength is no possible match. She smells stale sweat, stale cigarettes, and the acrid reek of partially digested alcohol. She retches, gags. The scrabbling fingers below have found their target and she recoils, bucks at the tearing, the violation, the shame. Tears force their way from her tightly squeezed eyelids. She tries again to scream, but it is strangled into a cruel muffled gasp. Her arms flail about uselessly at her sides, her hands grasping at everything, anything, nothing. She knows she is passing out: from the suffocating deadweight of his panting body pressing down on her small frame; from the endless searing pain; the heartbreaking hopelessness. She chokes, coughs and sputters to his every grunt.

Her scuffling fingers don't give in. They bang across the bedside table, smashing the two wine glasses and scattering a lamp and books, before miraculously wrapping themselves around the steely length of a ball-point pen. Her small child's fist barely makes a sound as it slaps upwards into the overbearing sweaty neck. The pen's tip grips, rips, slips almost effortlessly into the throbbing jugular. A hot and sticky flood erupts. It sprays the wall, splashes into her hair, and seeps into her eyes, so that when she opens them all the world seems red and dank and hellish. His legs jolt wildly as he gurgles, blindly rolling off the bed and slithering to the sleek marble floor. She can breathe, at last she can breathe! She sucks in the cool night air like it is salvation itself.

Throwing back the sheets, she staggers from his bed, staring aghast at his twitching body. It's terrible, horrible – and she lets out a single screaming howl, a banshee cry that echoes and reverberates down the hillside and out across the water. In the Aphrodite Hotel, in his bed, Demetri stirs, half awakened by a distant shriek, more animal than human.

The next morning she awakens early to her travel alarm. She feels strange. Dull and foggy, not fully in her body. Stumbling into the shower she is startled, frightened to see an intense swirl of red running from her hair. It circles the drain thickly, slowly, closing in like a fox around a doomed chicken. Is that? Oh my God, it is! But how? Where? Frantically she checks her head: surely there must be a hideous gash, some grave, terrible injury to account for so much dried blood. But she finds no wound.

'Goodbye, Abraxia,' she says as she hugs the old woman after breakfast. In all these years she has never bothered to learn the Greek language, but then neither has the old matriarch taken on English. Yet they've always known precisely what the other is saying. They have shared many an evening, sitting together in the dining room playing cards or watching the hazy TV. The hug is brief, but firm with friendship. Turning next to Demetri, she simply says, 'Demetri.' He takes her hand and makes a small bow. 'Next year, then,' he smiles, and she says, 'Yes indeed, I'll be back before you know it.' He studies her for a long moment with his cool, calm eyes. "I am wondering, in the middle of last night ...' But he stops, never finishes the sentence. 'As always, Miss Marjorie, your room will be waiting.'

Boarding the shuttle bus to the port to catch the 10am sailing back to the mainland, she nods to the bored driver who takes her ticket, ignoring her in his indifferent, cigarette-sucking slouch.

At the ferry she negotiates her rolling suitcase up the vehicle ramp, mindful of the boarding cars that pass all around her. Typically Greek, she muses, how they make no effort to divide off foot passengers from vehicles: a perilous game of dodge-'em. Safely aboard with fifteen minutes to departure she stands on the outside deck looking down at the picture-postcard scene below. The busy wharf and harbour, the shops, restaurants and hotels, and beyond, the craggy sun-baked bluffs and ridges.

A wailing duet cuts through the morning air, and she watches as two police cars, lights flashing, race past the port in the direction of San Stefano.

She slowly turns and makes her way inside to one of the ship's many cafés where she secures herself a seat. She knows the drill only too well. Sure enough, within minutes the trickle of Greek passengers arriving turns into a last-minute deluge. They stream onto the vessel, crowding and pushing into every nook and cranny, all talking at once, driving decibels into the stratosphere. In moments her café, and all others on the ferry, are teeming.

Watching all of this unfold is comforting – the soothing familiarity of it all. It's how she has led her life as far back as she can remember. Controlled, contained. It is this, as much as her fondness for Mykonos, San Stefano and the Aphrodite, that brings her back year after year. No surprises. Nothing alarming.

Everything routine.

Reliable.

Safe.

THE WHARF

TONIGHT I AM cooking the first of seven different dishes. Different, yet the same, since they are all covered by one simple generic term, based on the wonderful core ingredient around which everything else will revolve. Like the nucleus in the cell, the piece of grit that aggravates the pearl into being, the false illusion of sanctuary and calm that the eye of the storm brings as it passes over you – I'm talking the centre of things, the centre of life itself. The very place from which springs forth those three understated words of creation: In the beginning …

I know I am being somewhat obscure here but it is the mood I am in so please humour me. Because the question all of this is leading to is this: which came first? That's right, that all-time teaser. You see, you just can't call it. Go ahead and try: claim one, but recognise the equally compelling argument that will inevitably be made for the other. Nothing is sacrosanct, nothing absolute. Such a simple riddle really, to demonstrate that nothing – nothing! – can ever be taken for granted.

Personally, I don't truck with starting with the bird. Feathers, beak, scratching feet, all need to develop, grow from something. I'm too much an evolutionist to allow the finished article to just appear and be. No, let it emerge raw and unformed. Let it divide and multiply. Let it progress stage by stage to where, tonight, I can give credit where credit's due.

I shall enlarge upon the elliptical, orate upon the ovum, and certainly not avoid the ovoid. Let's take things, you and I, "ab ovo usque ad mala", to quote the good Roman, Horace: "from the egg right through to the apples." Because tonight, and for the next seven nights, I am cooking … 'eggs'.

If I was asked what one item of food I would take along with my must-hear discs to that mythical musical Radio 4 desert island, without question my answer would be eggs. Which is why I am taking the liberty, over this entire week, of presenting you with my favourite recipes for my favourite food. You see, over the years I have become more than a little adept in the egg-cooking department. Actually, false modesty does me no service here, let me state it unequivocally: I am decidedly good at cooking eggs.

It doesn't, I know, make up for my other shortcomings, but it is something I am strangely proud of, my prowess with the humble egg. So what follows is a simple step-by-step guide – how to cook, in a variety of useful ways, the perfect egg. A primer, if you will, for something primal. And forgive my tone if I seem at times to venture into the pedantic. When it comes to instructions on how to get your eggs just right, it's a serious business.

But before we even enter the kitchen, the first lesson to take onboard is this: wherever possible, use free-range, organic eggs. Why? Chicken welfare aside, this is the only way you can get to appreciate the amazing subtlety, texture and flavour of an egg. Cage-reared eggs are about as authentic as tinned spaghetti. So now, tonight, on this our first night together, without any further ado let Lesson Number One begin.

Soft-boiled Eggs

Take 2 eggs from the fridge. Place them gently into a small saucepan and just cover with cold water from the tap. Set over a full heat and bring to a full boil. Immediately remove the pan from the heat and allow it to stand for 3 minutes, no longer. During this time prepare and butter your toast. Serve your egg in an egg cup, pointy end upwards, the second egg resting on the plate or in a second cup. Strike off the top third with a clean hit of your knife. Dip your toast ends – ideally cut into fingers (or soldiers, as my militarily-inclined family was wont to say) – into the warm and runny yoke. Salt and pepper regularly as you eat your way down.

There it is, as simple as it gets. This is the trademark egg dish. Don't be beguiled into thinking something grander shows off your eggspertise. Undercook things and wobbly snot surrounds the golden core; overcook and any velvety coat-ability is lost. Nothing is worse than mangling your toast as you bounce it off a firm, unyielding yolk. No – experiment with your egg size and timings to get this one down first and foremost, over all the other recipes. Get your strike rate to ninety per cent plus – only then can you even begin to call yourself an egg chef.

Zero to seven – birth to boyhood. Apparently, the odds on just getting through from egg and sperm to newborn gooey baby on mother's breast are staggering. So I did well to arrive alive and healthy. No brothers or sisters, I was an only child. Father was a strict military man: 'Yes, sir … No, sir … Anything you say, sir' (just please don't come at me again, sir), and Mother was an alcoholic: 'Oh, is it five already? I could murder a drink!' (never mind the vodkas she'd been sucking on, on the quiet, since midday). So I might have picked better parents if I'd had the choice.

Living on a military base was no thing of joy – looking back it seems to me to have been some early form of gated community, but one that kept the riff-raff in, not out. Enlisted thugs: cloned, bullet-headed macho males who, perversely, were licensed to kill; or their all-superior, career-minded officers with their mannered ways and plummy speaking voices that belied an equally pervasive blood lust. And all of them either constantly shouting at their kids, or, as Father did, threatening them with a blistering, menacing silence.

Then there was the continual moving about. The security needs of this 'green and pleasant land', 'this sceptered isle', seemed to demand that our family shift homes six times between my birth and the end of the 1950s. My friends, like my young life, were transient and insubstantial. So I turned to make-believe ones: Jimmy-Joe, a boy my age who looked like me and was funny and could always make me laugh; a girl who was forever doing somersaults or running or standing on her head – a real tomboy – whom I named

Hayley (after Hayley Mills); and a monkey hand-puppet called Jacko. Jacko understood it when I was sad, he cried when I did, he hid when I did, and helped me rub away the soreness from the yellow, blue and brown marks on my bum, arms and legs.

In 1963 Father had an accident, was run over on base by a lorry. Ripped his right leg, right off. He died from the incessant loss of blood. Mother was devastated. I was confused. I wanted him back, but didn't. Wanted him back but changed, so I wouldn't be scared of him anymore. It was academic, he was gone. Mother now took to drinking like she meant it.

Poached Eggs

It is Tuesday tonight and for this evening's demonstration I'd like to move on to the obvious follow-up to last night's offering. Easier, in some ways, since you are able to see what's going on, and so are better able to control the outcome. I like to think of poached eggs as soft-boiled eggs but with the shell removed, so that the egg becomes capable of becoming so much more: for instance, evolving into such classics as Eggs Benedict or Eggs Florentine (more about these on another night). By being poached, the egg's potential has grown. It is more ambitious, more out there in the world, more visible. As long as you don't break the number one rule: never break the yolk. If you do, accept your fate and toss the egg out and start again.

And one more thing: forget about using so-called egg poachers, they're not the real thing. Perfectly round eggs, all looking exactly alike – ugh! – might as well be back on base. Besides, steaming is not poaching. Poaching is cooking slowly in a shallow liquid. Your egg needs to simply rest in slightly simmering water until cooked to perfection. Here's how.

Half-fill a frying pan with water to which you've added a good teaspoon of salt – this helps the egg white hold its shape until it sets. Forget vinegar, which does the same thing but can make the eggs go a bit rubbery and taint the taste. Heat the water until you see small bubbles forming on the pan's bottom, just beginning to break away and rise. If the water begins to boil, remove it from the heat and turn the control down a bit before continuing. You only want the gentlest of simmers.

Now carefully make a tiny break in the side of your egg (don't let it go in so far that it breaks the yolk sac) and holding the egg literally at the water's surface, ever-so-gently prise the broken shell open with your thumbs to allow the contents to slip delicately into the pan. Repeat for the second egg, placing it away from the first.

If you've taken the pan off the heat, return it, but watch that it never boils. Less is always more in this department. Prepare your toast. Check on the eggs' progress from time to time. When the whites look fully opaque and set, check how the yolks are faring. You can always slow things down by again briefly removing the frying pan from the heat. It's better that the yolks are undercooked at this stage, then all you need do is gently spoon some of the surrounding cooking water over them until their colour just dulls slightly, indicating that they've set on top. Serve on the buttered toast, using a spatula or slotted fish slice to lift each egg carefully from the water, allowing any water on the utensil and egg to drain off fully first. (Sodden toast under your perfectly poached eggs is an absolute no-no.)

Mother had to find work after Father died. She was trained for nothing and so turned to the one thing she had gained experience of through her twelve years of marriage: domestic cleaning. We shifted to London, settling in Hammersmith, where she found work in other people's homes six days a week. I didn't have a mother, not like before, but we did have a rented home that stayed put.

In the morning, before she left for work, Mother would leave out breakfast for me, and lunches she'd made up for me to take to school. But I fixed our tea at nights. It is during this time that I learned how to cook: mashed potatoes, boiled potatoes, chips, boiled cabbage, boiled carrots, stewing steak, the occasional chop or roast, crumbed fish, shepherd's pie, toad in the hole. We had a neighbour, ancient Mrs Hensley, who kept chickens in her backyard, and she used to let me feed them. In return, we enjoyed a steady supply of eggs, which I also began to cook at this time.

I enjoyed school, found learning easy, and finally, by not moving on, made real friends. I got on with life. While Mother, sadly, got on with her drinking. She was fired frequently for being drunk on the job, but always managed to find more work. She aged drastically, so that by the time I was fourteen and Sgt Pepper was teaching the band to play, Mother was grey-haired, walked with a noticeable stoop and was wizened well beyond her years. I remember once when we were out, a shopkeeper mistook her for my grandmother, neither of whom I knew, as all of my grandparents had died before I was born. Poor Mother.

Fried Eggs

Tonight's lesson might at first seem an affront. Surely anyone can fry an egg, right? In truth, anyone can murder an egg, and many do. They bubble, brown and blister the bottom and edges of the albumen until it goes shard-like and impenetrable. They harden the yolk to the consistency of meat, or manage to leave it haloed in slime: altogether revolting. More egg travesties occur through the simple act of frying than by any other method. Yet this is the one to get right because a well-fried egg is a reliable friend who will always turn up at a moment's notice, a thing of real pleasure, a thing of simple beauty.

Use either a non-stick pan (more about these later) or a heavy-based stainless-steel one. Avoid aluminium, it leaches into your food. You can use any fat to cook your fried eggs, but best steer away from strong flavours like dripping, bacon fat or olive oil, which mask the eggs' character. My recommendation is to use butter wherever possible – it enhances and enriches the taste. Put the butter in the pan and heat it. When the butter is melted and bubbling, but before it browns, break your eggs in, with as much care as you lavished on your poached eggs. Place the first egg to one side of the pan, and let it start to set before adding the second to the other side – you don't want the whites to overlap and merge. Keep the pan at a medium heat, and salt and pepper the eggs early on, while they're still cooking.

Now, here's the first of two important must-dos: cook your eggs in the style the Americans call 'over-easy'. This is the *coup de grace*. While the yolks are still very soft and the whites have only just finished setting, you want to carefully flip the egg and allow it to cook on its topside for a few moments – absolutely no more than 5–10 seconds. Have everything else you are planning to serve with the eggs ready and waiting so that this is the last thing you do. The trick to the maneuver is to slide your spatula or fish slice fully under the egg, and with your other hand, grip the frying pan handle and lift it off the heat. Holding the pan in front of you, raise and lower it in three short lifts: one, two – and on three, at the top of the lift, carry the egg up a little higher on your spatula and flip it delicately upside-down. It should land as the pan is traveling back downwards. Thus you are easing the egg's fall. This should prevent the yolk from breaking as it lands. Do the same with your second egg, by which time you want to be serving the first onto your plate.

Flip the egg over again as you plate it, so that the delicately sealed yolk is facing upwards. Complete your second egg similarly. If this seems too tricky, an alternative to flipping your eggs is to spoon hot butter from the pan over the yolks until their surfaces have just set.

The second must-do is to serve your fried friends with great companions. Fried eggs are endlessly gregarious. That's why they spit and cackle and talk so much – they're mates with everyone. They simply shine in the presence of others. Salty chips, buttery mushrooms, tasty fried tomatoes, crispy smoky bacon. Or go like the Americans, adding hash browns, fried onions, waffles or pancakes. The same holds true for an Asian spin, with fried rice or fried noodles. How about Mexican? Serve with refried beans, melted cheese and tortilla chips to have *huevos rancheros*. It's their amazing adaptability that makes fried eggs the brightest star in any culinary constellation.

These were my social years, when my mates were everything and held the fabric of my universe together. Mother began losing the plot when I was fifteen. By the time I reached my seventeenth birthday she was institutionalised. Unmitigated electro-convulsive therapy soon left her sad, addled brain ragged and torn, and her son unrecognised. I departed school with my A-levels and a need and determination to fend for myself in the world. With no real idea what I wanted to do I took work as an apprentice mechanic in a local garage. Frugality had been drummed into me for as long as I could remember, and it served me well now. I earned enough to pay the rent on the Hammersmith home and my way in the world. I was actually a good homemaker, having had so many years of practice.

Meanwhile, along with Peter Pecker (truly!), Simon Biddicombe, Julian Murphy and Nigel Anderson, I set about learning everything there was to learn about beer (Bass), cigarettes (Peter Stuyvesent), cars (Minis) and girls (any), in that order. You'd think having witnessed my mother's descent into alcohol-induced madness, I might have been wary of the demon drink, but no, I took to it like a duck to water. I always became highly convivial when drunk. I loved rolling out the stories and jokes, all that laughter surrounding me. It reassured me that I wasn't alone in the universe.

Cheese Soufflé

This may seem quite a jump, but I make it tonight for reasons that should become apparent. It is the fag end of a cold Thursday, pouring with rain outside. But my apartment is warm and cosy. Pink Floyd is playing in the background and I have a brandy snifter in hand. I, too, feel warm and cosy. Fifteen floors below me the Thames meanders off into the distance, the darkening scene punctured with lights like a wispy Whistler nocturne.

The trick with any soufflé is lightness. Never overbake it! The centre must remain moist and slightly soft. It is texture more than anything that makes this the great sensual dish it is. Preheat your oven to 190C (a bit lower for a fan oven) or Gas Mark 5. Grease the inside of an approximately 15cm (6-in) soufflé dish and set it aside.

Now make a good cheese sauce. Heat 25g (1oz) of

butter in a saucepan and stir in the same amount of plain white flour. Cook this roux briefly for up to a minute, stirring constantly, then add a quarter pint (120ml) of cold milk. Don't muck around adding it tiny amounts at a time in an effort to avoid lumps. Simply toss half the milk in and mix vigorously for a few moments with a manual hand-whisk until the heat begins to thicken it, then add the remainder and whisk again: so much easier and quicker. Allow it to bubble up and cook out for a minute, stirring all of the time. Remove from the heat and add a grated handful of good cheese: a nicely aged Cheddar is the classic, but Parmesan works a treat. Stir in 2 tbsps of double cream. This should cool your sauce slightly. Separate the yolks from the whites of 3 eggs and stir the yolks into the cheese sauce. Grace your sauce with a couple of twists of black pepper, a good pinch of salt and a hint of nutmeg, and mix everything well.

In a cold, dry bowl add the whites of 2 more eggs to the 3 egg whites you already have. Whisk until stiff, then beat 1 tbsp of this into the soufflé mixture to loosen it. Now you can fold in the remainder of the egg whites – and do fold, not stir! Use a dessertspoon, and with a cutting and turning motion gently incorporate everything together. Stirring will only knock out all of the air you've just spent minutes whisking into your egg whites. Remember, soufflés are all about air, and not a lot of substance. But that is their delight. Spoon this final mixture into the soufflé dish and bake for 25–30 minutes, until well risen and browned on top. Serve immediately.

Ah, the soufflé years. They began with Mother's passing, a relief to us both. What is it about our twenties? The ignorance of youth couched in the mantle of grown bodies and tantalising freedoms. We are totally new to this thing called adulthood, so what on earth gives us the right to believe we have any observations of real value to foist upon the world? I still cringe at the confident audacity with which I disseminated my smug opinions. Yet it is this very newness, this seeing of life through eyes as yet untainted, as yet un-world-weary, that lends us the urgency of our self-satisfying convictions. I was a naïve neophyte, endlessly ready to take risks. Light and pretentious, and of oh so little substance. What a time it was!

At age twenty-one I left Hammersmith, and the auto trade, and England. I travelled. Europe in the 1970s finally came up on the English radar as a place of possibilities — somehow less foreign than it had seemed before. Never British, oh, dear me no, but nevertheless a place anyone could venture into to experience broader aspects of life. Its sense of difference was its very appeal. My hair was well past my shoulders (take that, Father!), I was in brief love with Jenna, a blonde girl from Amsterdam, and we travelled in a Kombi convoy of VW vans, trailing cannabis clouds back and forth across borders. In the evenings we'd pull up in circles like wagon trains of the Wild West, and smoke, and drink cheap wine, and argue vehemently in an endless polemic over how to save whales from harpooning, forests from acid rain, Europe from reactor meltdowns, and the world from US versus Russian brinkmanship.

After Jenna came Alison. Allie hailed from Bristol, and truth to tell, it was her 'cities' that first attracted me to her. Then came Nancy, an American from Seattle. And did she ever! Nancy came and came and came. Sex held us together, literally. When we finally tired of doing it with each other in every conceivable fashion, we recognised there was nothing much else between us and we went our separate ways. By the early 1980s I was twenty-eight years old, tired of travel, tired of ranting, tired of fucking, tired of relationships. Tired of going everywhere and nowhere.

Eggs Benedict

There is something so sophisticated, understated and mature about Eggs Benedict. Take the humble poached egg and elevate it, almost by sleight of hand, to sublime greatness. It is almost too simple, seemingly little more than an act of assemblage. But this particular combination is the stuff of genius. It is essential you only use a top quality ham and, of course, a good Hollandaise sauce to top things off. You can buy prepared Hollandaise, but don't. We can do better.

Contrary to popular kitchen mythology, you can make your Hollandaise quickly and without fuss, using a blender or food processor. Melt 175g (6oz) of butter in a bowl in the microwave (or in a small saucepan on the stove top). Place in the blender the yolks from 3 large eggs along with 2 tbsps of Lemon Juice and mix well. Continue blending as you gradually pour in the melted butter until it is fully incorporated and the sauce is thickened. Season it with salt and pepper to taste, and put the blender aside wrapped in a tea towel to keep warm.

Now poach 2 eggs just as we did earlier in the week. Toast a split English muffin and butter both halves, and neatly cover (not smother) each with a few layers of thinly sliced ham (at room temperature, not straight from the fridge). Place your cooked eggs on top of the ham and immediately coat with the Hollandaise Sauce.

Variations on Eggs Benedict include replacing the ham with cooked spinach (Eggs Florentine) or smoked salmon (Eggs Royale). Both are wonderful, but in my opinion nothing really beats the original: a true classic.

The last years of my twenties up to halfway into my thirties were my time for settling down and, unexpectedly, getting stupidly rich. I was back again in London, at first sharing an apartment with two friends near Putney Bridge. One of them, Jimmie Bouzaid, worked as a creative in advertising, freelancing as a copywriter. He exhorted me to give it a go as well and threw the odd job my way. To the surprise of us both, I seemed to have a natural flair. Soon we were a duo in demand, hotshots bursting with ideas and confidence. It was the 1980s and yuppiedom was in full swing. Everyone was after big money, corporations appeared from nowhere, and wealth, on paper at least, spun freely around the city. *Miami Vice* showed us how to wear our suits, while the Iron Lady's northern ruthlessness only served to fuel our southern bullishness.

Jimmie and I formed AdWorks and began tugging some of that heady money-go-round our way. Before we knew it we were a trendy ad agency with a staff of thirty. Coke was the drug of choice, and we all danced headlong into the nights, enjoying every bit of the excess. Gluttons at the trough in a dizzy feeding frenzy – endlessly partying, as the song at the time said, like it was 1999. I bought cars, women, and a four-bedroom semi in Chelsea. Life was good, life was fast, life was humming.

Scrambled Eggs

Also out of the "80s came microwave ovens: the single greatest boon ever to the art of scrambled-egg cooking. You need never use a pan again! The beautifully creamy texture and intensity of egg flavour you'll get following tonight's instructions will make you a convert, believe me.

Melt 1 tbsp of butter in a microwave-safe bowl in the microwave. Swill the butter around to coat the sides. Break 2 eggs into the bowl and add 3-4 tsps of milk, or for a richer taste, single cream. Season with salt and pepper, then whisk everything with a fork until blended. Some say you should underdo the whisking so that something of the integrity of the egg white remains, but I disagree: you want a uniform whole.

Now place the bowl in the microwave and cook on high, at first, for anything from 30-60 seconds, depending on how powerful your microwave is. Stop when you see a ring of coagulating egg forming around the bowl's inside, and with your fork just gently pull this into the centre. From now on, the trick is to cook only in 15–30 second bursts – and, in between, to cut (not mash!) the setting egg into smaller lumps, always stirring them back into the remaining uncooked egg mixture. You may need to do this 5 or 6 times, but don't rush things.

Take greatest care when the cooking is nearing completion. Do not be tempted to do one burst too many: the eggs will keep on cooking afterwards due to residual heat, so you want to finish when they're still slightly underdone, with a creamy, eggy moistness over everything.

An unnecessary but totally delicious option, at this point, is to stir in a small handful of small-diced cheese chunks, say a good Cheddar, Gruyère or Parmesan (or even a blend of these, to taste). Season your eggs again lightly, give them a final stir and serve onto buttered toast, crumpets or English muffins, piling the curds nice and high. Comfort food par excellence!

Go at life hammer-and-tongs long enough and you'll lose direction and career full-speed into a cul-de-sac. If you're lucky, really lucky, you'll turn back on yourself and somehow just manage to avoid a splintering crash. I was really lucky. I now know how Mother felt, her brains a scrambled mish-mash.

When the bubble burst, Jimmie and I blamed each other. The fact was that we had both greedily snapped up one overnight-millionaire-client after another, believing in their own hype as much as they did. After all, we were their spin merchants, we had to believe the stories we were so readily selling to the market on their behalf. Neither of us ever expressed caution to each other, never once. We were bullet-proof. Why bring doubt and worry into the picture when you're having so much fun and making so much money? And we certainly weren't alone in a city that overplayed its hand time and again, ignoring the risks piling up above the dream like a bucket of shit balanced over a slightly ajar door. It was only my having fluked a terrific personal accountant – funnily enough, not our company's, I still don't know why – and an even better broker, that saved me a part of my fortune. Jimmie, however, lost it all. So much money up the nose and down the drain.

He despised me after the fall-out. But I didn't deserve his poisonous resentment at my luck in somehow riding out the shambolic demise of the dream decade. I've learned that deserving has nothing to do with life's tricks and turns. By the latter half of the 1990s I was a lonely, middle-aged forty-something has-been, with still enough capital in global investments that I needn't worry about earning a living ever again. Just as well – the burn-out has certainly taken its toll.

Omelette

Sunday night. Our final night, our final dish! I feel strangely moved. I've never liked the ending of things. I know they say that for every door that closes, a new one opens – it's just that so often we don't know what's on the other side.

We are using the same egg mixture as we did for scrambled eggs. Let me stress from the outset that if, for some reason, you don't own a non-stick frying pan, go out and get one immediately, they are a joy to work with. Teflon is truly God's great gift to omelette-makers.

A large frypan is best, as you want your egg mixture to have space to spread out, not sit in any great depth. Put the pan over a high heat and melt in 1 tbsp of butter, spreading it around with your spatula. When the pan is very hot, but before the butter browns, pour in the eggs and immediately tilt and rotate the pan so that the liquid swirls to cover the surface entirely.

Put the pan back on the heat, and, as the eggs quickly start to set on the bottom, carefully use the side of a fork to pull the cooked parts away from the edge in towards the pan's centre. Again tilt and swirl so that any uncooked mixture finds its way to the exposed pan bottom. Do this until there is no more uncooked egg to move around the pan.

Now give the omelette a good 30 seconds cooking time before taking the pan off the heat. At this point you want to add your filling or combination of fillings: cheese, diced ham, salami pieces, chopped onions, sliced tomatoes, diced cooked potato, whatever takes your fancy. Spread it evenly across the egg mixture. Two don'ts: don't put in fillings directly from the fridge, have them at least at room temperature; and don't overfill your omelette.

Interesting things, omelettes. They look nice on the outside (I trust that after following this recipe, yours will look stunning), but there are things they don't show. So much can be hidden in the folds. You taste, you discern, but you don't really see, not openly at any rate. You think you know what you're getting, but do you really?

Now comes the part – and it does take some dexterity – that will ensure your omelettes always end up plump and professional and perfect. Holding the pan directly in front of you, gently slide the spatula under one side and carefully fold one-third of the egg up over the filling, pressing it ever so gently into place with the spatula. Put the pan back on the heat for a few moments. Check that the underside surface has a nice mottling of brown and yellow, if it needs slightly more cooking time, give it a bit more, but don't overdo it.

The therapy has really helped. I hope Doc (he hates me calling him that but I can never resist) will believe me when he reads this. He's been an absolute pillar these past few years, really helping me hold it together. I know this will be a huge disappointment to him – not my recipes, they'll have him cooking eggs like a superstar in no time! It's just that at last I've come to see things clearly, as they really are. Shuffled my life into perspective. Hey Doc, you're always telling me that it's not about outcomes, it's about the journey. So don't get too hung up on this one, okay?

To finish your omelette, take the pan from the heat for a final time. Give it a few shakes to ensure that the omelette can slip about freely, and if need be ease the spatula around the edges or underneath to free it up.

You know, the "90s was such a strange decade. The world suddenly sped up, even faster, hard as that is to believe. So many changes! I truly never thought that I, an ex-adman, would drift out of step with the beat of the times – until the moment I realised with a jolt that I no longer had the slightest knowledge of the music scene of the day. The bands, the songs, the new categories and sub-categories of music, they'd all passed me by. Now, I'm just another aging classic-hits sort of guy, a forgettable statistic in the MOR demographic. How appalling. How incredibly sad.

Oh dear, I'm a bit all over the place tonight! The pills, the vodka – they've kicked in quicker than I'd planned. But I do so want you to get things right. Where was I?

Oh yes. Take the pan to your plate (pre-warmed, of course) and, controlling it with the handle, tilt it and shake slightly so that about a third of the unfolded side of egg slides out and sits proud of the pan's edge. Lower the pan to rest this bit of egg in the middle of the plate, and with a careful twist of your wrist, tilt the pan enough that the remaining omelette rolls out, folding over and on top of itself. Only the cooked underside should be showing now – everything is folded and tucked up neatly, complete with its hidden surprise. *Et voilà*, your masterpiece!

As the new millennium came and went, it became even more glaringly obvious to me that I was well and truly being left behind. Now, I fully recognise I've had my day. I am unnecessary – an irrelevance. I remain unmarried, never found the right woman, indeed never really tried. I have no family. No true friends – so many of them scattered after the coke ran out.

Money? Oh, I have money. And oodles of things. Assets. Sets for an ass! I'm a forlorn fifty-something has-been. My hairline is receding at a freakish pace, I wake up to piss two or three times a night, and my joints are starting to grind. My pubes are going grey and I'm alarmed to report that I've developed man-tits!

Funny thing, life. There's no recipe. You don't even know what ingredients you'll get. Just make it up as you go along. I'm out on the terrace of my Canary Wharf apartment, gazing, I must admit, with a certain fondness at this sprawling city. I do hope you enjoy my recipes. A strange l-egg-acy, perhaps, but who's to say how one should be remembered? Through the dusk, far below, I see the flickering lights of the DLR weaving its way over the Isle of Dogs. I stand here, leaning against the railing, as a knowing gust of wind buffets me, pulls at me. I shut my eyes against the vertigo. I could stay a little bit longer, but no, I really must fly. (Oh dear me, once an ad-man!)

And all the king's horses and all the king's men ...

ACKNOWLEDGMENTS

This collection of tales would not have come to fruition without the helpful input of many people. Author Fiona Farrell supplied that all-important initial spark and enthusiasm for my short story writing. My niece, Amanda Aarons, provided the much-needed digs during my year-long sabbatical in London. Jackie Cook and my fellow scribes in Nelson's STEM writing group gave me wonderful encouragement and support to finally get this book published. Kate Stone cast her invaluable professional editorial eye over everything. The team at CopyPress gave me their critical publishing expertise, including Suzanne North's excellent cover and layout design. And Sue, your endless belief in my creative endeavours remains my absolute bedrock. My heartfelt thanks goes out to you all.

ABOUT THE AUTHOR

J. W. Du Four lives in Nelson, New Zealand. Alongside his career as a creative director and copywriter in advertising, he has written many short stories, which have been published in magazines and anthologies. He has worked as a freelance journalist and magazine arts editor, while also writing for theatre and short films. His self-directed short, The Game, was a finalist in the Manhattan Short Film Festival. The City is his first published collection of short stories.